Strip Teaser

Naked Night's Book One

by

Ava Manello

Cover Design: Margreet Asselbergs

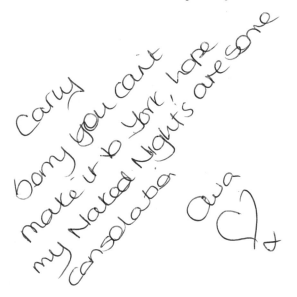

Copyright

Ava Manello
Strip Teaser

© 2014 Ava Manello

ISBN-13: 978-1500670535

ISBN-10:1500670537

KBK Publishing

ALL RIGHTS RESERVED. This book contains material protected under International and Federal Copyright Laws and Treaties. Any unauthorized reprint or use of this material is prohibited. No part of this book may be reproduced or transmitted in any form or by any means, electronic or mechanical, including photocopying, recording, or by any information storage and retrieval system without express written permission from the author / publisher.

DEDICATIONS

This book wouldn't have happened if certain people hadn't convinced me that I could go it alone. Thanks to K.T. Fisher, my partner in crime for starting me off on this crazy writing journey that I love.

Huge thanks to Emma Keating; she was with me every step of the way on this one. She suffered through hours and hours of research on YouTube with me, searching for the perfect tracks for the routines, and kept sending me lots of motivational pictures, but most of all, she believed I could do this and never let me forget it.

To my mother who still won't read my books, but does tell everyone that I write them now, we'll get there one day.

To my gorgeous daughter, who is proud of what I do and not ashamed to tell her friends. I think that's the biggest compliment she could give me. And she tells me every day that she loves me. I love you too baby girl xxx

ALSO AVAILABLE BY AVA MANELLO

Co-Authored with K.T. Fisher
Severed Angel (Severed MC 1)

Carnal Desire (Severed MC 2)

Severed Justice (Severed MC 3) Releasing 31st August

Available from all major eBook retailers now.

PROLOGUE

Alex

She gives me a look of warning as I leave the stage and head in her direction. Unlike the rest of the women on the front row, Sally's the only one not trying to attract my attention and screaming at me to pick them. The look changes to one of resigned acceptance as I take her hand and she reluctantly follows me back to the stage.

There's something about Sally that draws me to her. She's real for a start, not like the plastic Barbie dolls that normally show up for our performances. Eric will be pissed that I've picked her; he wants us to go for the loud, raucous girls that add to our performance, not a quiet girl like Sally. As far as I know this is the first time she's watched the performance from out front; she's hidden backstage the other nights. Eric wanted her to experience the show the same way the audience do. Well now she's going to get the full experience.

I guide her to the chair that's front and center of the stage. She sits primly, knees drawn together. I make a show of taking off my grey silk tie, slowly. The audience goes wild for the tie. Eric says it reminds them of Christian Grey, not that I knew who he was before I choreographed this routine, but it always gets a reaction. I unbutton my white shirt, one button at a time, drawing it out and letting my shirt hang open. The audience screams at the sight of my barely revealed abs.

I ease the tie through my hands slowly, almost caressing it, before gently drawing it sensuously across her face. I cover her eyes with the tie, securing it loosely at the back of her head. Moving in front of her, my back to the audience, I pretend to thrust my groin into her face. At the same time I lower the shirt down my back, revealing my strong shoulders inch by inch. Once it's off I ball it up, tossing it carelessly into the wings.

I turn to the audience, grinning and holding out the bottle of baby oil I just picked up. I make an elaborate show of the bottle and they scream in appreciation. I take one of Sally's hands in mine. It fits perfectly. Turning her hand so it's flat, palm up, I pour some of the oil into it, and then rub both her hands together. I move to stand in front of her, facing the audience, thrusting my groin at them. They scream. "Off. Off. Off." They're predictable after all. I take tiny steps backward until my legs are either side of Sally's, and then slowly lower myself into her lap. The blindfold heightens her senses, she may not be able to see me but she can feel me. She still utters a little murmur of surprise as I hover just above her lap. I reach behind me for her hands, bringing them round the front of my chiseled abs, and slowly, oh so slowly, I use her hands to rub the baby oil onto my chest. The lights glisten on the oil, making my upper body appear even more toned. "Just imagine your hands are mine." I whisper to her.

I do this performance nearly every night, I've had hundreds of women run their hands over me, but tonight something's different. Shit. This is actually arousing me. Do I show her what she's doing to me? I move her hands lower, slowly teasing the audience who encourage me with vulgar catcalls. "Get his cock out!" one girl screeches from the front row. The tempo of the music increases, becoming more sensual as I trace the V leading to the top of my waistband with her hands.

Eric allows us to decide just how far we go with this part of the act. Normally I stop here. Not tonight. I guide her hands to the belt buckle; she understands and releases the clasp. Next I guide her to draw the belt out, all our movements slow and sensual. I take the freed belt from her hand and throw it behind us on the stage. I reach for her hand again to release the button on my trousers. I hear the indrawn breath as she realizes this isn't quite the regular performance; one hand being drawn inside my waistband as the other releases the zipper. I want to tell her to touch me, that my cock won't bite her, but that kind of talk doesn't seem right with Sally. She's got too much class for that.

I use her hand to caress my length. Fuck. That feels so good through my boxers. I want this to be real, not an act. Her grip tightens gently, as much as I want to continue this, I can't.

The audience are egging her on, even more crude language spouting from their over glossed lips.

I stand quickly, startling Sally. Turning to face her I lower the waistband of my jeans an inch. On cue the screaming raises in volume. Another inch. Now they're shouting for me to "get em off" and to "get your cock out" My trousers are level with my boxers now, and I lower them both, inch by slow, teasing inch, until half of my arse is on display. I move a few steps closer to Sally, my groin level with her face. I grind a few times, stopping a whisper away from her lips. Oh God. The thought of those lips caressing my cock. I draw in a deep breath, calming my wayward thoughts. I'm desperately trying to get my head back into that neutral zone I use for performances.

I torment the audience a little more, pulling my trousers back up. Snap. I release them instantly, tossing them aside, and the screaming grows even more raucous if that were possible. Still facing Sally I pick up a towel. Holding it in front of me with one hand, I lower my boxers with the other. They fall, pooled around my feet. The screaming continues.

I step closer to Sally, the towel the only thing between her and me right now. I take one hand, placing it on an arse cheek, then repeat the action with her other hand. She understands what's needed and gently massages me. My cock gets even harder. At this point I'm supposed to thrust my towel-clad cock into her face. I can't. That feels wrong with Sally. I grind my hips, simulating the thrust, all the time wishing I could feel those perfect lips caressing me. I try to bring my mental state down from highly aroused to stage aroused; yes there's a difference.

I draw one of Sally's hands round to my front, placing it on my cock, holding the towel in place. The shock always makes them pull their hand back, well normally. There was one over eager fan who had a good grope the other night before releasing the towel. Sally performs as expected, pulling back her hand and allowing the towel to fall. The audience noise level is through the roof. One more hip thrust to finish off the performance, then I dramatically release Sally's blindfold. Her eyes go wide, and a smile lights up her face before she laughs out loud.

I turn to the audience; hands raised high, thrusting my hips towards them, along with my cock, still hidden in a Union Jack sock. I get a standing ovation.

I guide Sally back to her seat in the audience and thank her. The girls either side of her immediately begin calling her a lucky cow and asking what it was like. As I move back to the stage I don't miss the look in her eyes. I'm in for a shit load of trouble after the show, that's for sure.

You know what? It was totally worth it.

CHAPTER ONE

Sally - *a few days earlier*

I'm sitting on the edge of my bed, contemplating packing my suitcase and wondering how the hell I ended up in this predicament.

I'm an investigative journalist, granted it's only a small local paper, but I'm hopeful that one day one of the big boys will recognize my talent. There's a juicy little scandal at the local council and I was just about to get my teeth into it when my editor called me into his office this morning.

"Sally, my dear, how are you today?" Shit, he's being nice to me. This isn't good. Fred's an old school editor, he likes to bark and growl at his reporters. If he's being this nice then I'm either being made redundant or he's coming down with something.

I grunt a reply, which could mean anything. It's enough to satisfy him as he rattles on. "I've got a great assignment for you. You'll be starting it tonight so I'll need you to go pack. You can take the rest of the day off." I look at Fred, my face full of questions. What sort of assignment requires traveling? I was expecting to be doorstepping the local council offices until I got the dirt on the sleaze bag that's wasting public funds on holidays disguised as business trips. I'm sure it's just the tip of the iceberg.

"You're going on the road, Sally. It's all set up with their manager. You'll meet the guys on the bus." He picks up a piece of crumpled paper from his desk to check something, and then rushes on. "The bus will be at yours for 5pm."

What? Where? Why? The questions are rushing through my head at an alarming rate.

"What are you on about, Fred? I'm doing a piece on the Councilor. You know that. I haven't got time to be traveling anywhere. You'll have to give it to Rob, he's not got anything important on the go right now." I sit back, a smug grin on my face. There's no love lost between Rob and me. He's a prat, and that's me being nice. He thinks he's god's gift, and is constantly trying to get in my knickers. That's when he's not trying to sabotage my work.

Fred shifts uncomfortably in his seat. "Erm. Yes. Well."

"Spit it out, Fred. I need to get over to the council offices." I pretend to be bored, inspecting my manicure; if you can call chipped, month old polish a manicure.

"Well, Rob's not the man for the job in this case." He harrumphs again. "This job requires your particular set of skills." Now he looks downright embarrassed. What the hell am I getting shafted with here?

"What particular skills?" I narrow my eyes at Fred, who's now going an interesting shade of red.

"You're going on tour with some of our local performers." He smiles nervously.

Local performers? Crap! Tell me it's not the local Amateur Dramatic society. Someone shoot me now. He's got to be joking.

"Fred, need I remind you I'm an investigative reporter. That means I go out and investigate. I'm not a bloody reviewer, give it to someone else."

"There is no one else." He blusters.

"Of course there is, there's Rob, Kevin or Jack that I can think of off the top of my head." He shakes his head slowly.

"We need a woman for this one." At least he has the grace to look embarrassed; he should be, pulling this feminist crap on me. He must see the anger in my face as he rushes on. "It's a great opportunity for you Sally."

Fred rummages around on his desk then passes me a flyer. I take one look at it, before quickly standing and throwing it back in his face. "The Naked Night's," I screech. "You've got to be fucking kidding me!" I've always tried to remain professional in the office, but this time Fred's gone too far. "You want me to go on the road with a bunch of brawny, brainless male strippers. I'm not doing it." I turn to storm out of the office but Fred's next words cause me to pause.

"It's that or redundancy, Sally." Shit. I resume my seat. "You know advertising revenues are down. Our readers just don't care about council indiscretions; they hear it every night on the news. They want something more interesting. And the advertisers won't support a paper that's not interesting."

Interesting? I can think of plenty of words to describe a group of male strippers, and interesting isn't one of them.

"There's more isn't there?" I've never seen Fred look so uncomfortable and guilty. This must be bad.

"They're going on tour for eight weeks... and you'll be with them 24/7." My heart drops. I can't do this; surely he can't ask me to do this. Even my worst nightmare looks like a fairy tale in comparison to being asked to do this. "They're paying us a fortune in advertising."

Advertising? But I'm an investigative reporter. I dig for the truth. Then it dawns on me. If they're paying for the advertising this isn't even journalism. It's a bloody fluff piece, an advertorial disguised as an article. With my byline on it. I can't do it. I won't do it. Then I remember the bank statement that arrived this morning, with that horrible, scary looking overdrawn balance and the rent that's due at the end of the month.

"Fred, you can't ask me to do this, I'm a serious journalist." He doesn't reply. Shit. I'm really going to have to do this. "At least let me write it under a pen name?" I beg. With any luck no one will realize it's me, my future career will be safe, even if the next eight weeks of my life are doomed.

Fred agrees, and that's how I end up sitting on my bed, wondering what you're supposed to pack for eight weeks on the road with a bunch of male strippers.

I find my most practical, boring, yet comfortable clothes. Come to think of it, I'm not sure there's anything in my wardrobe that isn't practical and boring. It's not like I go out very often, and at work I prefer to blend into the background. Is that even going to be possible with these guys? I'm guessing wherever we go they'll be the center of attention.

I throw my toiletries in the top of the case. The clock tells me I've only got a few minutes to spare. Sure enough the doorbell sounds as I'm coming down the stairs. I grab my bag and keys and open the door.

"Sally?" He questions. I nod my head, too shocked to speak. "I'm Tiny; one of the guys, let me grab that case for you." Without giving me chance to answer he's taken my bag and started walking back to the minibus parked at the curb. A minibus? The guy in front of me is the size of a giant. He's so ripped I'm sure he has no neck left. How the hell will he fit on a minibus? And do they even make stripper outfits in his size?

I lock the door and follow meekly behind him, praying to an unseen God that he deliver me from the torment I'm about to suffer for the next eight weeks.

CHAPTER TWO

Sally

The minibus is better than I was expecting. It has large, comfortable leather seats and is slightly larger than the sort of minibus you'd hire for a hen night. I look around quickly, several of the seats are already filled with fairly hot looking men, but the seat at the front is empty so I move to sit there.

"Guys, shut up a minute." All conversation stops as everyone looks to Tiny, standing at the front of the bus. "This here is Sally; she's the reporter who's going to be stuck with us for the next eight weeks, so behave around her." There's a rather disinterested murmur from the guys, who ignore me and go back to whatever they were doing, be that listening to music, playing on their phones or what looks like a game of poker on one of the tables. Great. Seems like they want me here as little as I want to be here.

Tiny shrugs his shoulders, or I think he does, hard to tell when he's that big. "Sorry Sally. They're a pretty tight group and not used to dealing with women who aren't fans." He puts a comforting hand on my shoulder then turns to take a seat further down the bus. I'm about to sit down when I hear my name called. I turn to see a slightly older, but still attractive man pointing at the seat beside him.

"You'd better sit with me Sally; I'm Eric, the guy's manager and choreographer. I can explain what to expect over the next few weeks." Reluctantly I move to the seat he indicated. I'm a loner. I don't actively seek out company or conversation. I was hoping to sit on my own, and lose myself in my Kindle until we got to the hotel where we're staying tonight.

Eric stands, moving to kiss me on the cheek. I hold back a shudder. I'm not into public displays of affection. Who am I kidding? I'm not into private displays either. I take the seat next to him, fussing with my handbag unnecessarily to hide just how uncomfortable I'm feeling right now.

This is why I'm an investigative reporter. I get to create my stories from the sidelines, observing, rather than interacting with my subjects. I don't get close, because normally I'm not painting them in a very good light. They wouldn't be too pleased to know I was looking into their deep, dark secrets. I'll be honest; I'm not a people person. I keep to myself. I always have done. Instead of the life of the party, I'm the quiet one. I'm much happier with a book and my iTunes, than a beer and a disco.

I look around the minibus, just a quick glance, but it's enough to reinforce that I'm in my own idea of hell. The guys may be attractive, but they're loud, raucously so. There are beer cans on the tables, and from the sound of it they've already got through quite a few. I must grimace because Eric looks at me in sympathy. "They're a good bunch of guys, Sally, really." Is he trying to convince himself or me? He looks around the bus, affection clear in his face. "They're pretty grounded considering what they do. You'll be fine once you get to know them." He sounds sincere. "Let me tell you a little bit about them." He pulls the show's program to the center of the table.

The front cover shows the guys posing in tiny briefs against a deep red background, which only serves to emphasize the tanned and oiled bodies on display. They certainly look sculptured and fit. I look from the cover to the guys on the bus and can barely tell they're the same people. They look older and more serious in the photo compared to the relaxed and carefree guys on the minibus.

Eric opens it to the first page where there's a picture of a half-naked guy straddling a chair and begins the introductions.

"This is Alex; he's the quietest of the guys." As he speaks he indicates Alex sitting on his own on the other side of the bus. Alex has something about him, his blue eyes standing out on the page. I have a weakness for blue eyes. He's not as well built as Tiny, but then none of the guys are, but he definitely looks like he works out in the gym despite his slimmer physique. He has short, cropped dark hair, which seems to emphasize his eyes more. He's bare chested in the photo, and through the back of the chair there's a tantalizing hint of a V, leading down to his pale, torn denim jeans and bare feet. It's a hot photo, which even I can appreciate.

The next page shows Tiny, standing tall and proud wearing a navy suit and pale blue shirt that are hanging open to reveal his bare chest. I guess they call him Tiny as a play on his size. He's easily the largest guy here, I'm five seven and he towered above me. He has scruffy, tousled hair that looks like a woman has just been running her fingers through it. He's looking out of the corner of his eye at the photographer, and has a cheeky smile that's almost hidden in the several day old stubble on his face. Beards creep me out, but this looks just right. There's enough stubble that it looks deliberate, rather than a can't be bothered to shave effect, but not too much to put him in the realm of creepy hairy guy. He's well built but not fat, perhaps solid is a better description.

"This is Tiny, you've already met him. He's probably the peace keeper in the group, although he's in there with the rest of them when they party." Eric laughs.

The next page shows Guido. When Eric points to where he's sitting on the bus I can see his tan looks more orange than healthy glow. I'm guessing that with our typical English weather none of the tans are natural, but Guido's looks overly artificial. His chest in the photo is so smooth that I suspect it may be waxed as well.

"Guido's really called Gareth, and whilst he likes to pretend he's an Italian stallion he comes from Cleethorpes on the East Coast". Eric winks at me. I look back at Guido, his short dark hair and brown eyes could pass for Italian I guess in the photo, but in real life he just looks plastic and poseurish to me. He looks older than Alex, who I guessed was mid-twenties like me. I suspect he's nearer to hitting thirty.

The next page features Jackal. His head is practically shaved, just enough of a hint not to look bald. His tan seems darker than the others; I'm not sure if it's the tan causing the illusion or if he does have a more solid build than Guido. Looking at him on the bus, sitting next to Guido, his white T-shirt does seem to fill out more.

"This is Jackal or Jackie boy as we call him. He's a local boy, and is the newest member of the team."

Rick is wearing black boxers in his profile pic; they look much better than the skimpy briefs Guido and Jackal were sporting. He's got short dark hair, dark eyes and looks more serious than the other two. His hands are splayed back in the picture, almost as though he's pushing back from the backdrop of the photo. Like the others he's well built, has prominent abs and solid thighs.

Jonny has dark blonde hair, in contrast to the others, although his picture makes it look dark brown. His chiseled nose is prominent on his face, and he's got the most serious expression of them all, he's looking forward in his photo giving the illusion he's staring deep into my eyes.

The next page catches my attention as it's Eric's photo. It's a back view of him wearing a bright orange towel, slung low on his hips. The definition in his back and arms stands out. He looks like a bodybuilder compared to the rest of the guys. He's clearly older than them, but on the page he has a hell of a lot more character as well. He's darkly tanned in his photo, but sitting next to him now he looks a lot more natural. He's attractive in the way that a lot of older men are. I do think a lot of actors get better looking as they age. Sean Connery looks more attractive to me now than he ever did as a young James Bond. Perhaps it's maturity that does it.

I sweep my glance once more around the bus. I don't see male strippers; it looks more like a stag party to me.

Eric passes the brochure over to me. "Take this with you; it's got mini bios for each of them in there. It might help you to know a little bit about them before we start rehearsals." He pauses, thinking through his next words. "They're good guys deep down; don't be fooled by the personas they adopt for the fans. They'll probably show you that side of themselves for the next few days till they get to know you, just ignore them. Once they've got comfortable around you, you'll see a totally different side to them."

I don't want to get to know them. I don't want to be here in the first place.

"Thanks." I take the brochure reluctantly. I feel soiled already from this assignment. I just want to get to wherever we're going and scrub this dirty feeling away. I'm sure several of the girls in the office envy me right now, but I can't think of a worse way to spend the next eight weeks.

I discard the brochure on the table, pulling my Kindle out of my bag instead. I know it's rude of me, but I sit back and lose myself in the book I'm currently reading, anything to distract from this painful reality I've found myself in.

CHAPTER THREE

Alex

The guys are loud and boisterous as usual. I think they're playing cards. It's giving me a headache. Don't get me wrong; I get on well with them. I enjoy time in their company, but only in small doses.

Spending the next eight weeks touring the UK with them, even on a luxury minibus, is going to cause tempers to fray and friendships to suffer. If they behave like they normally do, then there'll be at least one physical altercation before we've reached the half way mark on the tour.

I can't say that becoming a male stripper is really how I envisaged my career path when I was asked what I wanted to do by the school careers officer. I smile when I think of what Ms. Thomas would say about the direction I've taken. She always told me I could do more if I only applied myself. All my teachers did, but she was the one who seemed the most frustrated by my lack of interest in academic pursuits.

I'd always been interested in drama and dance at school, although I never took part in the school performances. They were just too cheesy. I was lucky that my Dad supported me and encouraged me. He somehow found the money every month to send me to stage school, although I think he was a little disappointed that I didn't go down the professional footballer route. I had some talent there, but even I knew it wasn't enough to make a career out of it. I loved playing football, being part of a team, but I loved performing even more.

For years I was in the local pantomime, moving up from the junior ensemble to the seniors, performing alongside nationally acclaimed TV celebrities. My greatest pleasure though was performing in the youth groups and local amateur dramatic shows. There was camaraderie there. Yes, we had the odd diva, but for the most part, we had a laugh.

As with my football, I had talent, but not enough to make a decent living from it. I was dabbling with choreography as a possible career choice when I stumbled across a Naked Night's audition notice, and the rest is history.

I'm not as well built as Tiny and some of the other guys, but over the years in the gym I've kept myself fit and toned enough that I have a passable six-pack. The ladies scream for me, just not as loudly as they do for Guido and Jackal. It's not lack of dancing ability, without being conceited I'm a much better dancer than them. They just have charisma; their personality takes charge as soon as they step out on the stage. I don't have that confidence and arrogance. That charisma means the ladies forgive their lack of dancing prowess, or more likely just don't care.

I remember going home after the audition and wondering how the hell I was going to tell my Dad I was going to be a male stripper. The money was too good to turn down, and there was a possibility of some international travel if the show took off. I needn't have worried. My Dad's cool like that, as long as I was doing what I wanted to do, enjoying it and had enough money to get by on, he was happy.

Mum was the one who expressed concern over my choice. I think it was the thought of all those women ogling me. Let me tell you, my mother's not a prude. She reads loads of smut as she calls it, and loves it, often having a laugh with her friends over it. She just wasn't comfortable with the thought of her little boy being the object that her mummy porn friends would be lusting after. I've seen my Mum's Facebook timeline; it's disgusting. It's full of pictures of half-naked men, as are the book covers on her Goodreads account. Having seen that, I wasn't sure I was what the director would be looking for. Mum and her friends are into the chiseled, body builder types, covered in tattoos. I'm too slim for that, although Mum keeps telling me I'm lean not skinny. She's been to a few shows similar to the ones we'd be performing. It's fine for her and her mates to watch someone else's son perform, just not her baby boy. She's come round slowly, and even attended a few of my shows, although she never tells me when she'll be in the audience, knowing how uncomfortable that would make me.

She kept telling me that she wasn't seeing anything she hadn't seen before, reminding me that she'd been changing my diaper and bathing me from birth. Even my Gran came to one of my shows before she passed away. She loved it, and kept telling everyone who'd listen that she was my Gran. Bless her. Knowing she was in the audience really would have blown my mind. Luckily the first I knew about it was out front when we were signing autographs after the performance.

I tend to keep to myself when we're on tour. I'll join the guys for a drink on a free night, but performance nights most of them head off somewhere with one of the fans they've picked up. I think it's sleazy; a different woman every night, but Guido justifies it by saying he's performing a public service. Yeah, right. He's just a male whore. He's really not fussy who he takes home, although to be fair, he rarely takes them anywhere other than a dressing room or one of the toilets.

The guys have developed a brown bag rating. It's based on how many brown bags you'd have to put over her head to make her look attractive. It's demeaning and childish. I challenged Guido about it one day and now he's convinced the rest of the guys that I'm gay. I'm not; I just prefer to have some sort of emotional connection before I take a woman to bed. You don't find emotional connections on the road as a male stripper.

I'm drawn from my thoughts when we pull up outside a little bungalow and Tiny moves down the narrow aisle way of the bus. He just about fits through the door on the bus and it makes me smile. Out of all the guys Tiny is probably the one I am closest to. He's a giant in build, yet he's one of the gentlest souls I've ever met. He tends to be the peacekeeper amongst the group. Eric, our manager, is supposed to be the one in charge, but we all tend to listen to Tiny when it comes to disputes. It's amazing what they find to squabble over. Everything from position on stage, choice of song down to the color of G-strings!

Tiny's not been gone long when he returns to the bus followed by a woman who's hidden in his considerable shadow. He silences us quickly so he can introduce us to her. She's called Sally and she's a reporter. The poor bugger is stuck on this bus with us for the next eight weeks and she doesn't exactly look thrilled at the prospect.

I'm immediately drawn to her eyes. They're a stunning blue color, and stand out against the mane of golden brown hair. The inside of the minibus isn't quite light enough to gage the color properly but there appear to be golden highlights reflecting from the sun that's slowly setting outside the bus window.

She looks like she was going to take a seat at the front of the bus on her own, but Eric has called her over. She did well trying to hide the reluctance on her face; it was only there for a fraction of a second before she masked it. I chuckle silently; this is going to be an interesting few weeks.

The guys seem to have ignored her for now, Eric did warn us before we set off that she's off limits. We're not allowed to fraternize outside of her reporting is how he phrased it. He'd turned and looked Guido in the eye when he told us that meant no shagging! Guido had spluttered and tried to look innocent. That had the rest of us in stitches.

I'll admit to being intrigued by Sally. She's not what I expected. I'd thought any reporter prepared to travel with us guys would have to be feisty and brash. Sally looks more like a schoolteacher than a reporter.

I settle back in my seat and put my ear buds in, selecting a playlist on my phone. It's an eclectic mix of music that I can lose myself in. Everything from classical to hard rock. I close my eyes and relax as Cascada serenades me.

CHAPTER FOUR

Sally

The minibus is pulling into the car park of a Premier Inn. I guess it could be worse; we are in Blackpool after all. The Las Vegas of the North. It's funny, as a child I remember coming to Blackpool for the illuminations every October. Back then it was a bright, shiny and exciting place to visit. I came back a few years ago as an adult. We'd come for a colleague's hen night and it was the opposite of everything I remembered. The cheap guesthouse we stayed in was so dirty I'd had to go out and buy some cleaning stuff before I'd dared set foot in the shower. Nowadays Blackpool just looks grim and dirty to me, a far cry from my childhood memories. It's a mecca for stag nights and hen parties. I'm sure with that sort of audience the boys will have a sell out show at the Blackpool Opera House.

From what I can see most of the venues seat between two to three thousand each. I break out into a shiver at the thought of two to three thousand bawdy, loud women lusting and leering.

I'm drawn back to the present when Eric starts handing out the room assignments; he's pairing the guys up. Luckily for me I have a room to myself. The thought of sharing with anyone, let alone a man is abhorrent to me. I'm far too private a person.

By the time we've all made it into reception and received our keys, our bags are there waiting for us. I thank Dan, the driver, as he hands me my case. I'm achy after the journey, I'm not used to being sat in one place for so long. I'm normally much more active, and it's made me tired and grouchy. I suppose it's not the journey that made me grouchy if I'm honest with myself; it's the job I've been assigned that's responsible for this miserable mood.

Eric suggests we all meet down in the bar in half an hour for something to eat. I'd rather hide away with the room service menu but agree to join them - this time. I suppose now is as good a time as any to break the ice and get to know a little more about everyone.

The lift is too small for us all to fit in together, and as my room is on the first floor I decide to take the stairs. Tiny is struggling to fit his large frame and his bag into the lift, much to the amusement of the others. Cursing mildly he gives in and moves over to the stairway door, we both reach for the handle at the same time. Tiny gives me a smile that lights up his whole face.

"Ladies first, which floor are you on, I'll carry your bag up for you if you like." I'm about to refuse, and insist I can carry my own bags, when I realize he's just being a gentleman. That's something I'm not used to. Don't get me wrong, I'm not a feminist by any means, but I do like to do things for myself. The men I'm used to always seem to want something in return for any token act of kindness. There's a vibe about Tiny that immediately tells me that's not the case with him. I hand over my bag, thanking him. It turns out we're in rooms next to each other. He hands me my bag once he's made sure I get in my room okay. "Let me know when you're ready and I'll escort you down to the bar." He gives me that warm smile of his again, before unlocking his own room and disappearing from sight.

I'm confused. Tiny's not what I expected from a male stripper. He's polite, courteous and seems like a respectful guy. Then again, what experience do I have of male strippers? Just a preconceived notion in my head. I hope the rest of the guys are like him, but perhaps I'm asking too much. Only time will tell.

With having to be down in the bar soon I haven't got time to unpack yet. I take a brief glance around the room; if you've been in one Premier Inn you've been in them all. They're affordable, basically equipped but clean and comfortable. I quickly wash my face in the bathroom, then try and tidy up my hair. It will have to do for now. I've got a room with a bath and I'm wondering how early I can make my excuses from dinner and get back up here and soak. I'd rather have stayed in my room, had room service, a warm bath and finished the hot book on my Kindle, but I can't. I look at my weary reflection, give myself a pep talk and put on my game face, before heading to knock on Tiny's door so he can escort me down to dinner.

***

I can't believe how much food this lot just devoured. You'd think they hadn't been fed in a week. They'd ordered starters, steaks, baked potatoes, salad and desserts. The servings were more than generous and I'd struggled to eat half my pasta bake, having declined any other courses. My plate was empty by the time the waitress came to clear the table as Tiny kept leaning over and eating a forkful at a time.

"How can you lot eat so much and not have fat bellies?" I laughed, as we all started to rise from the table to head into the bar.

"Because we spend hours in the gym to tone up." he replied with a pained expression. "That and the routines and rehearsals keep us in shape." He followed this with a hip thrust causing me to laugh out loud. This set the rest of them off, and they sashayed over to the bar with a series of thrusts, bumps and grinds. I could see the disgusted faces on some of the older residents of the hotel, and blushed to my roots. This caused Tiny to guffaw loudly.

"If you're that embarrassed over a few simple moves, you're never going to be able to handle our full routines." he smirked. "Is Sally joining us for rehearsals, Eric?"

Eric looked at me with sympathy, but then made me feel even worse by letting me know he was expecting to see me there so I could get a real feel for the show, and how much work went into it.

I was about to make my excuses and head back to my room when Tiny grabbed my arm and dragged me over to one of the leather sofas in the bar area, dragging me down to sit beside him. That wouldn't have been too bad, we just about fit on there together, but Guido decided to squeeze in on my other side.

I like my personal space. There's nothing worse than feeling hemmed in, and having to hold my elbows close into my sides to avoid touching the person next to me. Given the choice, I'd have been in one of the leather tub chairs on my own. Well, given the choice I'd have been alone in my bedroom, but that didn't look like it was going to happen.

I tried not to look too uncomfortable but being squeezed in between these two guys, and not having a clue what the conversation was about, it wasn't easy.

It soon became obvious that not everyone had Tiny's manners and respectful nature, nor did they seem bothered that I was there, listening to them. I grew more and more uncomfortable as Guido, Jackal, Rick and Jonny shared stories of sexual conquests they'd made at the end of the last show.

I cringed at the crudeness they displayed. Eric looked on like a proud father figure. Alex and Tiny weren't joining in, they seemed to be having a separate conversation to the others, but as Alex was on the other side of Tiny to me, I couldn't hear what was being said.

I'd pretty much zoned out on them all when I was nudged by Tiny. "Sally? Did you hear Alex ask you about the gym?" I looked over to Alex who'd apparently asked me a question.

"I'm sorry Alex, I was miles away. What about the gym?"

"I just wondered what your normal fitness regime was. Did you want to come to the gym with me and Tiny before rehearsals tomorrow?" Alex asked quietly.

"I normally run most mornings on my own. I'll probably get up early and do that, Thanks anyway." I tried to decline as politely as I could. Like everything else in my life, running was something I did on my own.

"You need to come to the gym and let us give you a proper workout." Tiny grinned.

Yeah. Right. There was no way I was going to a gym, sweating my socks off, and looking like death warmed up in front of these two hunks. I'm fit, but I'm not toned. I'm a plodder more than a runner. I run to free my mind. Some of my best stories have been plotted out whilst running. I plug in my iTunes, close out the world and just free my mind when I run. When I get back from my runs I'm a sweaty, red-faced mess. The best part of running for me is the shower at the end of it. I was about to politely decline when Alex leaned closer.

"Come on Sally, it will be a nice change not to have to look at Tiny's ugly mug all morning." his smile was so warm and genuine. "It'll just be the three of us." He looked over at the rest of the guys. "They'll still be in their beds after spending all night in the bar."

I actually gave it a moment's thought. I'd been considering hitting the gym lately, booking a session with a private trainer to try and up my fitness levels. I'd not been to the gym for months despite paying for it, and even then I'd not done more than hit up the treadmill before going to see my sports physio who was located in the same building.

"Okay, just this once." As soon as I said the words I regretted them. The good thing about my gym was the anonymity. It was rare that I saw the same faces, I didn't know them, and they didn't know me. I was in and out. Before I could change my mind and utter the words Tiny stopped me.

"No backing out now, Sally." he laughed. "I can see you trying to work out how to get out of it. I'll pick you up at 8am." Alex and Tiny grinned at each other, before high fiving. Damn. I was stuck with it now. With any luck they'd be off on the weights and I could find a treadmill in a dark corner on my own.

I'd exceeded my social quota for the month, never mind the day. I really needed some alone time, so feigning a yawn I excused myself from the group. Tiny and Alex, ever the gentlemen, stood up as I rose from my seat. The others were so lost in conversation I don't think they even noticed me leaving. Tiny offered to escort me to my room, but I declined. It was sweet of him, but it's not like I could get lost between the bar and the first floor room I was in.

I scurried off as quickly as I could, welcoming the quiet and solitude of my room when I reached it.

I drew a hot, relaxing bath, picked up my Kindle and lost myself in my book for the rest of the evening.

CHAPTER FIVE

Sally

I stayed up late last night reading the book on my Kindle. It's a weakness of mine, once I've started a book I don't like to put it down and this one had gripped me. The knock on the door at 8am is more than unwelcome, as was the alarm going off on my phone a half hour earlier.

I've put on my running kit, it's all I've brought with me and it will have to do for the gym. It's months since I was last at one and I have a feeling Alex and Tiny won't let me get away with hiding in a corner on a treadmill.

The gym is within walking distance of where we're staying so we decide to use the walk as part of our warm up. I cringe when we get there, as it's one of the huge chain gyms. No doubt it will be full of toned women in their fancy outfits all jogging gently on the treadmill, fearful of breaking out in a sweat and messing up their perfect hair. Look, I never said I was a happy morning person now did I. Until I've had at least my second cup of coffee I am best left alone; actually I'm probably best left alone most of the time.

Tiny hands me a bottle of cold water he's grabbed from reception, and as I feared, the place is full of gym bunnies. Typical. There are several guys here as well, but none of them are as attractive as the ones that are currently by my side. Alex points to a couple of treadmills that are well away from the others.

"I'm going to start you off gently, just a five minute warm up for the cardio." He reaches over and starts the machine. "Each minute I want you to up the speed by just one level." he requests. This is a little alien to me, when I get on the treadmill I tend to go straight into my run. He's set me off at a very gentle stroll pace. Perhaps this isn't going to be as hard as I thought. I look to my side and see he's walking on his treadmill as well. Alex catches me watching him and gives me a smile. He has the most gorgeous smile; his eyes light up with it. I'm a sucker for a nice smile. I look around for Tiny and see he's headed over to the weights area. I hope they're not expecting me to lift weights. I don't mind toning up but I really don't want to bulk up.

Before I know it the five minutes of warm up on the treadmill have passed and Alex guides me to an area away from the machines. There are a couple of exercise mats and some kettle bells. I give him a questioning look.

"I'm going to give you some exercises to help keep you toned, but first we need to do some active stretches." What the hell is an active stretch? It turns out to be very similar to the static stretches I do before or after a run but has more movement in it, squatting up and down and moving my arms a lot more. Alex explains that it's to keep the cardio element going.

"I'll start you off with the viper, it's fairly simple to use." He smiles as he walks over to an equipment rack. What the hell is a viper? The only viper I know is a deadly snake or a hot guy from Top Gun. Somehow, I doubt very much he's bringing me the hot guy from Top Gun though. I'm right. Alex heads back over with a long, fat tube with handles. The closest thing I can think of is one of the weapons they use to knock each other off the raised stage in the TV show Gladiators. I snicker. Alex doesn't look amused.

Alex demonstrates swinging the viper up in front of me, twisting it in the air then sweeping it back down through my legs, I have to twist it again for the upward pass. It's kind of like a figure of eight motion. It's a good job he's counting for me, as I have no idea how to remember the move and the count at the same time.

"Last two." he smiles. "There, that wasn't so bad now was it?" He's right. It actually felt pretty easy. I'm surprised he didn't ask me to do a second set.

Alex replaces the viper in the equipment stand and to my horror moves over to the kettle bells. I'm relieved when he picks up what looks to be the lightest one. The relief doesn't last long though as this bitch is heavy. This time he has me squatting, which feels immensely uncomfortable. It's not a natural position. I have to lift and twist with the kettle bell. When he calls last two I am so relieved. This was not a piece of gym equipment I ever want to see again.

Next up is the medicine ball. It looks heavier than the kettle bell, but to my relief it's not. Again he has me squatting, lifting and twisting with it. That was a hell of a lot easier. I almost suggested swapping it for a heavier weight but kept my mouth shut.

There's what looks to be a little table in the corner and Alex demonstrates the stepping action he'd like me to use. That is not a step; it's a bloody huge step. It resembles my coffee table at home it's that high. I have to raise one leg onto it in a stepping motion then step up and twist the other leg across in front of me before stepping back to the floor and repeating the action with my other leg. This is about the same time I realize just how bloody uncoordinated I am. Several times I start off with the wrong leg, in the end I just leave Alex to do the count and I purely concentrate on telling myself lead left or lead right. He makes me do two sets of these.

By the time we get to the weird looking machine in the weights corner I'm feeling fine, not what I expected from a private training session. I have no idea what the machine is called but Alex sets the pin in the right weight for me. I contemplate asking for a heavier weight after the first pull, but suspect he's going to get me to do multiple repetitions so leave it for now. I stand sideways and pull the handle on a long string across and up my body, adding in a twisting half turn. I'm sure that exercise is supposed to hurt but so far I feel fine. When we've done a few repetitions of this he leads me over to the cross trainer for the cool down. This is the opposite of the treadmill, I start off at a high speed and every minute slow it down a little more. The static stretches at the end are the only part of the routine I'm familiar with. They're the same ones I do at the end of my run.

When I look up at the clock I see we've been here an hour. It feels like only a fraction of that time. Despite my reservations I didn't hate the session. Granted I didn't like it either, but it could have been a lot worse. I could quite happily go for a run now. I won't. I'm not a total glutton for punishment.

"How do you feel?" Tiny comes up behind me, startling me.

"I'm fine. It wasn't as hard as I expected."

"I was watching you, you're not as unfit as you led us to believe." he laughs.

"I guess I'm not as unfit as I led myself to believe." This guy is just so comfortable to be around. Well, outside of the gym perhaps. The lascivious looks from some of the gym bunnies are making me feel really uncomfortable. They're eying Alex and Tiny up as though they were offerings on a menu. Tiny catches one woman watching him and winks at her. At least she has the good grace to blush, knowing she's been caught ogling.

Tiny looks back to me. "It's my turn to train you tomorrow. I'm going to see the sparkle in your eyes, have your cheeks flush red, and sweat running down your body as I work you so hard you'll ache everywhere the day after because of me". Shit. That sounded erotic. I really do need to stop reading those bloody books on my Kindle.

"I won't ache tomorrow, I just did my stretches." I say confidently. I've been running long enough to know when my body will ache and when it won't. Tiny and Alex exchange a look and burst out laughing.

"Just make sure you have some Ibuprofen on hand." Alex smirks. "Just in case." I give them both my most sarcastic look and skip over to the changing room to collect my bag. I'll shower back at the hotel.

CHAPTER SIX

Alex

I had fun at the gym with Sally this morning. She's got a great sense of humor, she's attractive, and I just feel so comfortable in her company. On tour artificial and over made up women constantly surround me. They say what they think we want to hear in order to get into our beds. This isn't how I like my sex. I need a connection, not just some quick grope in a corridor or bathroom stall. Luckily for many of our fans some of the guys are more than happy to oblige.

Tiny and I are the only ones who don't get drawn in. Eric has the occasional dalliance, but at least he tends to choose the more normal amongst the fans. Guido is such a whore; he really doesn't care who he beds. I'm surprised his cock hasn't fallen off yet considering some of the places he's shoved it over the last year. He seems to think that wrapping it will keep him safe. I don't think he quite comprehends that baby oil and condoms don't actually mix well. Still, that's his lesson to learn.

Jackal, Jonny and Rick aren't quite the man whores that Guido is, but they're not that far behind.

Aside from the lack of morals they're a good team to work with. They show up for rehearsal on time, they pick up the moves I show them without too many mistakes, and we have a laugh together. Off the stage they're pretty normal guys.

We've arrived at the theater for rehearsal. It always feels weird being on stage in front of an empty auditorium. It feels kind of creepy. Most of the theaters we play in are really old; they have a history of memories and I'm pretty sure some of them have the odd ghost as well.

I'm trying to work on a new routine before the guys join me on stage. It's a solo I'll be doing whilst the rest of the guys do a costume change. We quickly discovered the audience doesn't like gaps between performances. It's the Christian Grey look again. I come on stage in ripped faded denim jeans and a white shirt hanging loosely over the top of them.

I was too embarrassed to walk into a sex shop for the accessories I needed so I went online. All I can say is thank god Lovehoney deliver in plain cardboard boxes. The last thing I wanted was my post lady knowing what she was delivering.

In one hand I'm holding a pair of shiny silver handcuffs, in the other I have a black and silver flogger. The metallic silver strands catch the light on stage when it moves. They had a suede one or a rubber one as well, but this looked the most effective for the performance.

The intro to Snow Patrol "The Lightning Strike - What if this storm ends" comes on and I start to move easily across the stage, more ballet style than anything. How's that for attention to detail, not only did I buy the FSOG sex toys, I researched the playlist as well. As the beat increases and the singer stops, I toss the cuffs away and ease off my shirt, which I also discard. As the song moves on and the words come back I use the flogger, crossing my arm over my body I hit my shoulder with it, then switch to the other side.

There are hardly any words to the song; it's a much more visual experience than aural. My moves are graceful; I'm trying my best to look hot and tortured. As the music slows and quiets I draw the flogger down my chest, sinking to my knees. I've kept my jeans on, and done the routine bare chested.

I catch movement in the wings. It's Sally. She's looking at me almost in awe.

"That was beautiful.," she gasps. "I've never heard that song before."

"Thanks. I'm not sure if I'll be able to use it in the show though."

"Why?" I forget Sally hasn't seen our show yet. She'll understand soon enough. It's not the show as much as the audience that will be a problem. "I'm not sure they'll like me keeping my trousers on." I answer her honestly. Sally blushes. For all her bravado she's actually quite shy.

"I guess that's why it wasn't what I was expecting. I didn't think you'd be a dancer." She starts to look embarrassed at her words. "I mean, well, I mean. Oh crap, I don't know how to say it."

I laugh to ease the situation. "It's okay, I know what you mean. You didn't expect us to be graceful perhaps?" I suggest. Sally nods her head.

"Yeah. I think that's it. I thought it would be heavy rock beats, tacky songs and you lot ripping your clothes off." She's still blushing slightly. It looks good on her.

"It is with some groups, but Eric is happy for me to try some different stuff. We can't all be Magic Mike." I smile. I confess to having watched the movie to see what all the fuss was about but hadn't been that enamored of it. The story line was too dark and depressing to go alongside the stripping action.

"Besides, this routine is to fill in after one of the strip ones and give the guys chance to change for the big finale. I want to quieten it down a bit for the audience so they can really get all heated up again later."

"It's very sensual. I assume it's a play on Fifty Shades?" she questions, looking down at the ripped jeans and the flogger that's hanging carelessly in my hand. When her eyes catch sight of the flogger there's a spark in her eye that's quickly extinguished. I wonder. I can't let my thoughts go there though. Eric would kill me. He's told us all how important it is that Sally writes a positive series of articles about the tour. We need the bookings.

I walk over to the rear of the stage to pick up my discarded shirt and the cuffs. Sally's eyes are instantly drawn to the cuffs and that sparkle is back. Shit. A flash of her with them fastened around those perfect wrists, securing her to my bed flashes through my head. I feel a stir in my pants as I think about what I could do to her, what I want to do to her. I'd love to go there but I daren't. Eric would have my balls for it.

Sally

What's that phrase that I read in that MC book the other day? Foo Foo Clenching. That's it. Shit, I know exactly what it means now. Watching Alex on that stage sure as hell made my foo foo clench. It was sensual and erotic. I hope Eric let's him add the routine to the show, but perhaps he's right. Maybe it's too sensual and not lewd enough for the type of audience the Naked Night's will attract.

The guys aren't what I expected. Well, mostly. Alex and Tiny are the total opposite of who and what I thought they'd be. The other four are slightly more stereotypical with their fake tans and larger than life egos, yet most of the time they're pleasant and polite.

I'm still not comfortable around any of them. I'm not used to the company of men, who am I kidding, I'm not used to the company of anyone. I'm so much a loner it's silly. For all my twenty-four years I'd be a crazy cat lady already if my landlord allowed pets. Animals are so much simpler. With people come expectations, disappointments and letdowns.

I don't need a man. What use are they anyway. They certainly aren't like the guys you read about in books. I'd love to experience book sex one day but I'm convinced it doesn't exist. Instead my experiences consist of a quick fumble under the covers, a couple of grunts and groans from him then he turns over, farts and goes to sleep regardless of whether I'm satisfied or not.

Did I mention that's with the lights off? I'm too ashamed of my body to risk the lights on, and let's be honest; the naked male body sure as hell isn't very attractive. I much prefer men to keep their clothes on. The Naked Night's do have some pretty impressive abs though; as long as they keep their boxers on we'll be fine.

I can hear Eric calling the rest of the guys to the stage for a full rehearsal. They need to mark out positions and stuff like that. I know, they had all these technical words for it but it went straight over my head.

Grabbing my notebook and a stool I position myself in the wings, out of the way and start recording my thoughts as they run through their routine. That's easier said than done when

Alex comes on stage as my foo foo clenching starts all over again. Down girl, down!

CHAPTER SEVEN

Sally

The show wasn't quite what I was expecting; then again do I know what that was really? I've watched The Full Monty and Magic Mike and even old videos of The Chippendales on YouTube. This was classier than those. The guys can all dance, well most of them can. Guido does a good impression of it, but to my critical eye his timing was slightly off. It didn't seem to be noticeable to the hyenas in the audience though. That wasn't what I expected, it was worse, much, much worse.

Last night, hiding in the wings, I was ashamed to be female. The audience was feral in its behavior. Their language and suggestions were beyond crude. Is there really a need to act that way? I've seen raucous hen parties but last night made them look like a church potluck in comparison.

It seemed to be the larger the girl the more outrageously she behaved. Guido lapped it up. He seemed to be the most popular member of the Night's at the meet and greet after the show. I don't know where he sloped off to but he left the room several times, each time with a different fan in tow.

Either he doesn't know how to use his god given equipment or they weren't doing it for him as he always came back fairly quickly on his own. I cringe at the memory.

I'm not a prude. I read erotic books for a start. Okay, maybe I am, as I could never picture myself going off for a quickie with a male stripper I'd just met. I may not be a fan of sex but I do believe there needs to be some sort of connection between me and the man I jump into bed with. I'm exaggerating again. No one has ever jumped in my bed. I've only had a couple of partners and neither of them was interested in more than a quick vanilla session before rolling over and taking the quilt with them. In books the men all grunt and groan and use dirty language. Does that happen in real life? I wouldn't know what a multiple orgasm was if it came and slapped me in the face to introduce itself, then again I wouldn't know what an orgasm from sex was either.

Growing up sex wasn't something that was talked about in our house. It was considered not just taboo but dirty as well. You've never seen a remote pointed so quickly at a TV screen as it was when a bedroom scene came on. To make it worse I went to an all girls' school. No, not the plaid mini skirt and short white blouse all girls school. An all girls school full of bitchiness, laziness and a total lack of interest in education. A couple of the teachers battled through the apathy for those of us who showed any aptitude, but it was obvious their soul wasn't in it any more. I did okay at school, I was always top of the class, but I was woefully prepared for what came after. That first day walking into the college was a nightmare. I was the only one there from my school, the others deciding not to continue into further education. I didn't recognize the kids I'd gone to junior school with anymore. It was as though those last five years apart from them had been spent in solitary. I came to college full of eager anticipation and left that first day full of disappointment. The lack of interest from my fellow pupils had kept me back in terms of education, and I discovered that I had zero social skills to go with my lack of knowledge. It's possibly why I prefer working alone now. I quickly discovered what life feels like on the outside, realizing that it's safer to stay there than to try and become part of an established clique.

The five years I'd spent away from boys may as well have been fifty. Even the ones I'd shared junior school with were strangers to me. Suddenly it mattered not who you were but who your partner was. You were judged no longer on personality, but purely on pulling power. This strange new world was too much for me and I retreated further into my shell.

Looking back I'd say both the men I'd slept with were immature. The first took my virginity in a drunken one-night episode on a foreign holiday, mere hours after our first meeting. It was such an unforgettable experience I'm not sure it counted. What should have been the sharing of something special turned into a quickie mistake. Alcohol is not my friend. It imbibes a false confidence that leads people into embarrassing situations. You only have to look at the behavior at the staff Xmas party to see examples of it.

The second man flattered his way into my bed and my heart. Looking back I wasn't in love with him. I was in love with the idea of being in love. We settled into a boring and normal routine. Yes I tried to spice things up from time to time buying beautiful french knickers and bra sets and even using the erotic novels I've read as reference material, but it was always in vain. I could have gone on forever, lost on that aimless track. He proposed on my birthday. Well, what he thought was my birthday. Three years of being together and he couldn't even get the date of my birthday right. He took me to a cheap Italian restaurant, part of a chain, fed me lukewarm spaghetti then leaned over the table soaking his tie in the left over tomato sauce from his pasta, as he dramatically opened the jeweler's box to reveal a gaudy and cheap ring. He really didn't know me at all. I'm not into show. His proposal never once included mention of love. It seemed to be more a description of me changing my life to become the proper little solicitors wife, I sat there, looking at this man who shared my bed for the last year and a bit and for the first time I really saw him. My future looked gloomy at his side. I politely declined his offer, and suggested that I didn't think we were right for each other after all. I stood from the table, grabbed my bag and left. His chin was practically hitting the table as he spluttered on about me never finding anyone as good as him in my future.

That ended over a year ago, and whilst I may have foo foo clenching moment's, I never act on them. Look where it leads. Sweaty socks, dirty linen and saying goodbye to the remote control don't loom large on my horizon anymore and

I'm grateful. I miss companionship, but I don't miss sex. My friend Sasha tells me that's because I was doing it wrong. I guess we'll never know.

I glance at my iPhone on the nightstand. It's three am. I've been lost reading a book again. I loved this one, there's nothing better than a book where you keep telling yourself you'll stop reading after this one last chapter and before you know it those taunting words 'The End' bring your reading session to a halt. I decide to go to the bathroom and brush my teeth before calling it a night. That's when it hits me.

I try to move from the bed to find my whole body has almost seized up. Holy crap. Everything hurts. I think back to the gym session with Alex this morning, or was it yesterday morning? At the time it had felt fairly easy, there were points where I felt I could have done more but if I suggested it Alex just smirked at me in that knowing way of his. Now I know why.

My back feels like it's seized into one solid bone. There's no flexibility there at all. I don't get it. I've never hurt like this when I've pushed myself running, and that's when I realize. My general fitness routine consists of running, and only running. My legs may be used to the abuse but the rest of my body isn't. These aches and pains let me know about muscles I didn't know I had. I rise slowly, shuffling along the floor to the bathroom like a geriatric old lady.

Turns out getting to the bathroom was the easy part, trying to lift myself from the toilet presents a whole new challenge. What should have taken moment's turns into an almost epic trial just to lift myself from the toilet seat. I remove some ibuprofen from my toilet bag and swallow them down with a mouthful of disgusting lukewarm tap water.

We'll be on the road again after breakfast, as comfortable as that mini bus seat is, I'm not looking forward to it. I groan as I look back at the phone and see it's now three thirty in the morning. I need to try and sleep as Tiny promised to call for me on his way down to breakfast at eight. I lower myself to the bed, grimacing as my tender back hits the mattress.

Right at this moment in time I'm plotting how to write an article on the Naked Night's that will not only make them look bad, I'm wishing I was an erotic author so I could kill Alex off slowly and painfully in my next book. Thinking of Alex wasn't such a good idea. I picture that cheeky grin of his and those blue eyes and go to sleep feeling horny as hell.

CHAPTER EIGHT

Sally

Tiny laughed when he saw the state of me as I opened the door to him. I was shuffling along like an old lady, a grimace permanently attached to my face. Every single part of me ached. I'd discovered muscles I hadn't known existed.

He took pity on me and let me use the lift to get down to the dining room for breakfast. The thought of even attempting stairs this morning brought me out in a cold sweat.

Breakfast was spent as the butt of the guy's jokes. They thought it was hilarious, going on about me being a pussy. I'd never thought before just how much work these guys put into staying fit. Now I could see that a great part of each day for them is spent either in the gym or practicing routines, they're always on the go.

We'll be on the road again after lunch, and I think this journey is at least a couple of hours long, we're heading to Leeds next. A couple of hours in a minibus right now are more like my idea of hell than heaven. I'm not sure I can concentrate on a book even, never mind making a start on the article I have to submit for the paper this week. I still haven't come up with an angle I want to cover, though perhaps the fitness levels wouldn't be a bad place to start. I can take a couple of shots of the guys in their gym gear and that should appease my editor.

The guys are going to use the morning to head back to the gym but Alex offers to stay behind and give me a sports massage. Cue more eye rolling and kinky comments from across the table.

"Ignore these losers Sally, it's just a sports massage. It'll loosen you up a little, ready for your next workout tomorrow." Alex whispers at my side. That was definitely bad timing as I spit my mouthful of coffee across the table towards a rather disgruntled Jackal.

"Next workout? You're kidding me right? No way Jose, I'm not setting foot in a gym with you again." I sound like a petulant five year old right now. My aching muscles send up a silent cheer.

"You're not with Alex tomorrow, you're with me." Tiny gives me a triumphant grin. Shit. If I can't handle a routine that Alex set me then there's no hope of me surviving a session with Tiny. I've seen him working out. He lifts some serious weights.

"Tiny, I'm not with anyone tomorrow. If I can walk by then I might go for a run." I pause. "On my own." I quickly add before either of them can offer to accompany me.

"You can't run on your own, it's not safe." Rick tells me. I look over at him and see he's serious.

"You're joking me right? I always run on my own." My inner feminist is bristling at the turn the conversation is taking.

"You shouldn't." Rick advises. "Trust me there are some absolute nutters out there. And don't forget you're not on home ground either. We can't let you run a new route on your own. If you won't go to the gym then one of us will go with you."

I put my coffee cup down on the table, taking a moment and pause, carefully considering the wording of my reply.

"I am not going to the gym, and I am not running with you guys. I'm a big girl in case you haven't noticed. I know how to take care of myself and I'm not stupid." My voice is rising slightly and the old couple at the table beside us looks over to see what's happening. I try and calm myself down before carrying on. "I'm not the plastic Barbie dolls you guys are used to, I don't need protecting, I don't need mollycoddling and I sure as heck don't need to be told what I can and can't do thank you very much." This is the point where what I wanted to do is stand and push my chair back and stalk from the room. Of course, in my head this was a grand exit. In reality I can only just about lift myself from the chair and shuffle from the room in a very ungraceful and extremely undramatic fashion. The table behind me erupts in laughter, and I hear Jonny. "That told you Rick!" before he too lets out a loud guffaw.

The lift door is about to close when it's rudely pulled open again and Alex slips in beside me. I give him my best dirty look.

"Don't be giving me that prissy face Sally. I'm here to help you. Come back to my room and I'll give you that sports massage I was offering earlier. Trust me, you'll feel much better after it." He looks genuine in his offer; I'll give him that.

"Do I look like the kind of girl that goes back to a strippers room?" I sneer. Alex's face falls. That was cruel and uncalled for on my part.

"Do I behave like a typical male stripper?" Alex sounds sad. "I'm not trying to jump your bones you know Sally, just offering to help ease a bit of that pain you're walking around with."

Now I feel like a total bitch. "I'm sorry Alex, I am in pain and that pain is making me more bitchy than normal." I shrug my shoulders then groan as even that hurts this morning. "I guess it wouldn't hurt to try. Thank you."

Alex's room is a few doors down from mine and I'm surprised at how tidy it is. I try and keep my room tidy but living out of a suitcase isn't ideal and these places never seem to have room to unpack properly.

Alex gestures to the bed. "I'll go grab a towel, can you strip down to your underwear, it will make it a bit easier for me." I can't help it. Alex asking me to strip off brings a blush to my face, even if it was a perfectly reasonable request. He returns from the bathroom and places a towel on top of the bed. I'm struggling to get my t-shirt off; my arms don't seem to be able to lift high enough to get it over my head this morning. Before I know what's happening Alex is in front of me. "Can I help?" he gestures to the hem of my t-shirt. I shrug in acceptance.

Alex takes hold of the hem and starts to lift the shirt slowly, his fingers graze my flesh and it feels erotic. It's like a lover's touch. Gentle. It's maybe my imagination but it suddenly feels rather warm in here.

"You need help with these too?" he asks, gesturing to my jeans. I nod, momentarily speechless. My jeans are soon folded on the counter beside my shirt. I shuffle to the bed and groan as I try and lay down on my front.

"This might be a little cold." Alex warns me. Despite the warning, I still gasp as the cold liquid hits my shoulders. "You're going to feel a lot more pressure than you would on a relaxation massage." He advises me. "You need the pressure to release the tension from the muscles."

"It's okay, I've had sports massages before." I'm not a wuss; I can handle the pain that goes with a sports massage. "They're a regular part of my routine when I'm training for races." I advise.

"What races have you done?" he asks. I bite my lip before replying. He's started on my shoulders and I can feel from the pressure he's exerting just how tense they are.

"Mostly 10k's but I've done a half marathon and London Marathon once." He presses more firmly on a tense area and I can't help swearing. He laughs.

"Sorry, I'll warn you before I do that again. How was London? I've always wanted to do that but I've never been able to get in on the ballot."

The conversation distracts me for the next hour as he works his way all over my body. This room is definitely too warm. I can feel the sheen on my skin. Despite the pressure he was applying it started to feel quite erotic when he was working on the back of my legs. His hands are so soft; there were moments where it felt like he was caressing my skin. They didn't last long though as the next second he'd be applying pressure. All I can say is it's a good job there's no swear box in the room or I'd be bankrupt by the time we finished. I'll say this for him; he's good at sports massage. I've been to a few until I found the one I use now and he's at the upper range of ability.

I sense his hands leaving my skin, this time though they don't return. "You can get up now, how does that feel?" he asks. I can't tell him how it really feels. I'm disappointed truth be told. Despite the pressure, his touch was gentle and welcome. I miss it.

I ease myself off the bed, grateful for the increase in my range of movement. Where before everything ached, now it feels much looser and just slightly tender.

"When was the last time you had a massage?" he questions. "Your back was pretty knotted up, much more than it should have been after that simple routine yesterday."

"It's been a while." I confess. "I kind of got involved in this article I'm working on and kept putting it off." We start chatting about the corrupt councilor and how I really want to be working on that article. He sounds interested in what I'm saying, and from his responses I can tell he's educated. I don't notice that I'm still sat here in nothing more than my underwear until Alex reaches over to pat my arm. It's as if he suddenly realizes I'm not dressed as well. He looks embarrassed and tries to hide it by gathering up the towel and bottle of lotion and dashing off into the bathroom. I manage to dress myself without assistance this time.

"Thank you for that, it's made a huge difference." The atmosphere between us has changed. Where moments before we were chatting animatedly and comfortable in each other's presence, suddenly we're awkward with each other.

"That's okay, think nothing of it," he mumbles. "I'll see you down at the bus later?"

I nod, no longer capable of getting words out. I'm like a bloody love struck teenager suddenly. I fumble with the door handle and breathe a sigh of relief when I find myself outside in the hallway, the door safely shut behind me.

There's a chuckle from the doorway across the hall. I look up to see Tiny watching me.

"Don't worry Sally, he has that effect on all the women." I huff, turning my back on him and walk off in the direction of my room just a few doors away. Yes, walk. That massage did wonders for my shuffling gait.

As if Alex has an effect on me, that's nonsense I tell myself. I'm not into guys like him. And that's when that stupid inner voice pipes up. "Who do you think you're kidding?" It's right. There's something about Alex that gets me all worked up and hot inside. But I won't give into it. I'm here to do a job and nothing else. My inner voice pipes up again. "Damn shame."

CHAPTER NINE

Alex

I was all hot and bothered after massaging Sally this morning. I'm still frustrated. Jerking off in a cold shower didn't give me much relief. I feel like a horny teenage boy again. I like Sally, there's something honest about her. Being out on the road isn't conducive to a relationship though. The only one of us who has a woman at home is Tiny. Jonny had a girlfriend for a while, and whilst he behaved himself, she couldn't get over the jealousy, and constantly accused him of cheating. There are plenty of opportunities to go off with someone after a show; several someone's in fact, some of these girls aren't fussy. Becoming a male whore never has appealed to me, and aside from that I have taste. Let's be honest, there are very few classy women in the audience at these events; not that I've come across anyway.

We've spent the afternoon, or what feels like most of it, on the minibus travelling to Kingston upon Hull. We've not got a show tonight so we can have a rest, then we've got two shows in two nights at two different venues. At least this time they're less than an hour apart. I hate the overnight trips where we have to try and sleep on the minibus as the next venue is so far away. Eric's pretty good at keeping the venues within travelling distance of each other, but every now and then he gets a chance at a bigger venue and we have to travel for it.

The minibus pulls up outside yet another Travelodge. Because they all look alike you forget which town you're in sometimes. That said, all looking alike is a good thing, as at least we know we've got a certain standard rather than some of the guesthouses we used to take over when we first started. Eric quickly realized he had no tolerance for nosy old landladies who tutted and disapproved of our career choices. Now we stick to nice, safe, anonymous hotels.

The guys are milling around in the lobby working out what they want to do this evening. From the sound of it they're going bar hopping. Great. Not my scene at all. Luckily Tiny comes to the rescue.

"If you don't fancy going on a bar crawl with this bunch of reprobates why not come to the cinema with me and Alex tonight, Sally? The Odeon is in walking distance of here." Sally looks uncertain.

"What were you thinking of watching Tiny?" I question. "I'm not sitting through another bloody chick flick with you; I can't stand watching you cry." I laugh and it's good to hear Sally join in.

"There's that 80's thing, Walking on Sunshine, or there's Transformers if you want a little action." he glances up from his phone where he's obviously checking out the cinema listing. "Most of them start between eight and half past so we can choose when we get there, and it gives us time to get some food into these losers to soak up all that alcohol they're going to wreck their bodies with later." He affectionately ruffles Jackal's hair, knowing how much it winds him up.

"You guys are more like brothers at times." She smiles. Just a few days on the road with us and I can tell we've broken down some of her misconceptions. "Okay, I'm up for it, I haven't been to watch a movie in forever, it'll make a nice change. Thanks."

We've not long finished dinner before Guido has pulled. Pulled might be a bit over enthusiastic, she practically jumped on him. I'm sat on one of the leather sofas in the bar with Tiny, Eric and Sally watching the scene unfold at the bar.

"This should be entertaining," mutters Eric. He expressly forbade us from messing around with girls in front of Sally. He's got no chance. It's not the guys he needed to warn; it's the over enthusiastic fans at the theaters where we perform. Sally looks up to see what he's talking about and her face stiffens with a look of disgust. Yep, this is going to be interesting alright.

Sally

The skanky blonde at the bar is all over Guido. If she's trying to do an impression of a limpet she's doing a good job of it. Her artificially inflated chest is pressed against his shirt and she's practically wrapped one leg around his. Her slightly too small body con dress is stretching at the seams as it is, without the leg moves. Guido doesn't look uncomfortable at all though, if anything he's lapping it up. Her painted nails are playing with the top button of his shirt as she undoes one, then two of the buttons and draws her nail across his naked flesh. If that's supposed to be seductive, it's not. Someone pass me a sick bag before I throw up.

She tosses her backcombed mane over her shoulder, reaching in to whisper in his ear. The way his smile lights up his face you'd have thought she'd just told a small child it was Christmas morning. Guido turns and high fives Jonny before mumbling something I can't hear, and leaving the bar, the girl still attached wherever she can to his body like some slimy suckered octopus. I shiver with disgust.

Tiny and Alex just exchange raised eyebrows and shrug. It's obviously standard behavior for them to witness. Jonny, Jackal and Rick are still drinking at the bar. Looks like Miss Barbie left a few of her friends behind. Despite their best attempts the guys aren't looking overly eager to follow in Guido's footsteps.

"Does this happen often?" I ask. Shit. I can't help the distaste that showed in my voice.

"Too often." Eric answers. He looks pissed.

"We all get propositioned, a lot." Tiny answers me. "Difference is that Guido's really the only one to take advantage of it. He's got a bit of a reputation with the ladies as some sort of Italian Stallion." I smother a laugh. I'm pretty sure from what I already know that Guido aka Gareth from Cleethorpes has no Italian ancestry in him whatsoever.

"The problem is doing this sort of show attracts the wrong sort of women." Alex is thoughtful before he continues. "They're not the sort that are looking for a relationship. They're after a quick fix. They just want to go back to their mates and say they slept with a male stripper. It's kudos for them. They're worse than guys for bragging rights." Alex sounds so disappointed.

"So you don't take advantage when it's offered?" I sneer. I can't believe I just asked that. I'm never normally this aggressive in a social conversation.

"No, I don't." He huffs. "I have dignity; and last time I looked, I have taste. I'd rather meet someone like you." Alex stops talking suddenly. Was that a compliment he just paid me or something more? I'm no good at picking up on things like this. Whilst I'd like it to be more than a compliment I tell my inner voice to shut up and simmer down. He must have just been trying to be polite.

"I don't think in the time I've known Alex I've ever seen him go off with anyone," laughs Tiny. Alex gets up to go to the bar, taking our empty glasses with him. "The guys are convinced he's gay, and to be honest, I have my suspicions as well." Tiny adds in a whisper next to my ear. Just my luck. The first decent guy I come across in ages and he's batting for the other side. That would explain why I feel so comfortable around him though; he's not a threat.

"What about you then, Tiny? You sample the goods?" He looks affronted, and pulls a photo out from his wallet. It's crumpled from use but it shows him and a petite but very attractive brunette with their arms around each other, smiling broadly at the camera.

"Nope, I have my girl at home, and I'm a good boy." He smiles, passing me the photo for closer inspection. "This is Alison, my fiancée. She's a teaching assistant. We're getting married next year when I quit." Tiny looks so proud when he's talking to me, but the word quit brings Eric's attention back to the conversation. He doesn't look pleased.

"You can't quit Tiny, the group needs you. Let me talk to her and see if I can get her to change her mind." Eric pleads.

"It's not Alison's choice, Eric. It's mine. I've been doing this since before I met her. I'm getting too old for this shit. If it's not the traveling it's the rehearsals, if it's not the rehearsals it's being objectified by that bunch of screaming harlots." There's just a hint of anger in Tiny's voice. It's subtle, but I hear it. I get the impression this is a conversation that's been repeated one too many times for him.

Eric shrugs his shoulders in defeat, not answering. It feels uncomfortable. Alex returns with the drinks and looks at us, as if wondering why we're not talking to each other. I try and break the silence by telling Tiny how pretty Alison is. We talk a little longer before I excuse myself to go to the bathroom.

There's a stall that's occupied when I walk in and I can hear muttering and mumbling as though the occupant is talking to themselves. I'm about to lock the cubicle door and make use of the convenience when I hear the conversation in the stall next to me. I stop, shocked and slowly back out.

"What do you mean you've finished? You haven't even put it in yet." That one's a female voice.

"I'm holding a condom full of come, of course I've bloody finished." the male voice retorts. I almost gasp out loud when I realize they're having sex in a Travelodge bathroom stall. Aside from it being so public they're not the roomiest place I can think of. Why wouldn't they just go upstairs to a room?
"You selfish prick" the female voice screeches. "You didn't even get me off, and your cock's that fucking small I'd need a microscope to find it."

"Well if you weren't such a loose slag you'd have felt me come." he retorts. I recognize the male voice now. It's Guido!

There's more shuffling and movement inside the stall and I hear the unmistakable sound of a zipper fastening. I have to get out of here, fast.

I manage to make it out of the bathroom just in time. I hide in a corner behind a potted plant, waiting for them to pass and head back into the bar. All the while they're grumbling and muttering at each other.

My need to pee has deserted me so I head back to the sofa, taking my seat next to Tiny. I've just picked up my glass and taken a mouthful when I hear the screechy voice talking to her friends. I spit my drink across the table when she utters the immortal words "Best fucking cock I've had in my fanny in month's girls."

Tiny looks on in puzzlement as I sit there, laughing so hard there are tears pouring down my face.

CHAPTER TEN

Sally

Alex and Tiny wouldn't let it rest until I'd told them what I'd been laughing so hard about. I struggled to get the words out for laughing. I'm sorry, but this girl made the women on the Jeremy Kyle show look classy; and that's saying something. She stood in that toilet complaining about Guido's lack of sexual prowess and in the next breath is telling her friends how good he was. Either she's a bold faced liar or she really has had some bad sexual experiences.

"That's what it's all about." Tiny looks sad as he says this. "These girls are just after bragging rights. I think some of them would run a mile if we asked them for their phone number." he smiles.

"Yeah." Alex agrees. "And that daft bugger just goes along with it every night." he looks over to Guido who's deep in conversation with Jackal.

"Come on, grab your jacket. The cinema's just a short walk from here. Let's go see if we can find something Tiny won't cry over tonight." Alex pushes on Tiny's shoulder. You can see the affection on both their faces. They have a much closer bond than the other guys.

As we pass the bar on our way out the girls are still cackling amongst themselves, a couple of them throwing longing glances towards Guido. I wonder how they'd handle finding out for themselves that their friend was as loose with the truth as she is with her morals.

Tiny casually throws his arm around my shoulder as we walk. Alex is on the other side of me. Despite Tiny being closer, it's Alex's warmth that I can feel. There's a glow down that side of my body, and I feel drawn to him. After Tiny's earlier declaration that Alex is gay I need to calm down my libido and quickly. I can settle for friendship. My mind might be okay with that but the tingling between my legs tells me my body has other ideas.

***

The movie was okay; I can't say that I remember much of it. I was too conscious of Alex sitting by my side the whole time. Tiny bought the biggest tub of popcorn he could find, plonked me on the seat in the middle along with the popcorn and proceeded to eat most of it single handed. Alex reached for it at the same time as me once. There was a tingling as our hands touched, and I pulled mine away shocked. Alex gave me a slightly puzzled expression, but carried on slowly munching away; oblivious to the turmoil my body was in.

The walk back to the hotel was pretty quiet. Tiny cracked the silence with the odd joke from the movie but other than that we kept to our own thoughts.

"You got the bike sorted for tomorrow?" Tiny looks over at Alex. I prick my ears up a little.

"Yeah, the guy I spoke to is bringing it to the theater in the afternoon. He's got a red and black Harley Road King. Should look good with the leather and the lights." Now I'm intrigued.

Tiny obviously notices my interest and puts me out of my misery. "Alex has a routine planned using a bike on the stage tomorrow night. You coming to rehearsals to watch?" Alex, a bike and leather? I think they'd struggle to keep me away.

CHAPTER ELEVEN

Sally

I watched Alex rehearse this afternoon and his performance looked great, but tonight I've moved out of the wings to stand at the back of the auditorium so I can see his act properly. Jed, the owner of the bike, is standing next to me. He's been a bag of nerves all day; that's his precious baby up on that stage after all. He's polished every millimeter of chrome and the red paintwork sparkles in the stage lighting.

Right now the stage is in darkness, as the gentle guitar strum intro to AC/DC's Highway to Hell is played through the sound system. As the rest of the music kicks in there's a flash of fire before a single spot hits the stage. Alex is revealed; standing astride the bike in the sexiest black leather outfit I've ever seen.

The bike is sideways on to the audience, secured in place with the center stand. Alex is standing atop it, facing the audience, legs spread wide for balance. At the next beat he leaps down to the front of the stage.

The black leather jacket is open revealing glimpses of his toned abs, and his arse, oh god his arse, is revealed in tight black boxer briefs whilst his legs are covered in black leather chaps. My jaw drops. He looked hot backstage just before he went on, but in this setting, the crowd has gone crazy. My knickers just got a little bit wet as well.

"Fuckin' ell." Jed mutters at the side of me. "Bet you wish I looked like that in me leathers." He smiles at me before turning back to watch the performance. I grin, he's fifty if he's a day and I don't think if he was half that age he'd look as hot as Alex right now.

Alex thrusts and dances his way around the bike. I can't believe how agile he is in the leather; at times he kneels down throwing his hips forward. At the chorus he caresses the bike like it was some kind of lover. He straddles the front wheel, grinding his hips towards the forks and handlebars. He turns his back to the audience, drawing the leather jacket off one shoulder then the next and teasing it down his back. In just one shrug it's gone and cast aside. The audience screams at him to get the rest of his kit off. They might be bloody heathens, but I can see a real art in this performance. You can tell Alex has a dancing background.

He lays down flat to the stage, humping up and down suggestively with his groin. I can't help but wonder how that would feel if he was in bed with me. I give myself a gentle shake to remind myself that's never going to happen. Now I'm jealous of the lucky bloke that gets to experience that.

At the next chorus he moves to the back wheel of the bike, grinding against the seat. God, I wish I were that leather seat right now. He struts around the stage, pumping and gyrating his hips, circling closer to the front as he goes. At times he falls to the floor, snaking his way across the front of the stage using his hips.

At the words 'and I'm going down' the lights go off as Alex drops to his knees, his head in his hands, a single spot highlighting him on the stage with the shadow of the bike in the background. He's glistening all over, his chest glowing with sweat. He stands slowly, shakes himself down and in one swift move pulls off the chaps to 'on the highway to hell'. The crowd stands and screams and the light goes out, leaving the stage in darkness.

"Wow." Jed is lost for words. "I'm a bloke and that was bloody hot." he sighs.

CHAPTER TWELVE

Sally

I toss my Kindle aside in frustration. After watching Alex perform last night I just can't get my mind off him. It means I can't concentrate on the book I'm trying to read either. Every time something sensual happens to the characters in the book I find myself imagining that it's happening to Alex and me instead. Face it girl, he bats for the other side, it's never going to happen.

I look at the clock on my phone. Tiny's decided he's taking me to the gym today as I've refused to let Alex show me any more routines. He's promised to be gentle with me but for some reason I'm taking that promise with a pinch of salt.

The knock at the door shifts me from my stupor. Time to head to the gym.

***

So much for Tiny going easy on me, this is ten times harder than the routine that Alex put me through. We start off on the treadmill like last time but from the first set of cardiac stretches it's different. I never realized Tiny had such an evil streak. It's not just that the routines harder, making me really break out in a sweat, a lot of the moves are just humiliating.

Alex had me swinging that viper tube thing up over my head, but no, Tiny wants me to do the viper crawl, possibly the most embarrassing position I've ever found my body in at a gym. I have to lean over the viper as it points away ahead of me, my hands flat to the floor either side of it, my arse in the air and my feet on the ground. I grab the viper and throw it forward, not that 8 kilos goes very far in this position, then crawl towards it and repeat the motion until I'm at the end of the sectioned off area. Now when babies crawl they have their knees on the floor, which would be more natural than this arse up position I'm in, and it takes a moment or two for my brain to actually work out how to move. I breathe in a sigh of satisfaction at the end until he tells me I have to go back the same way. Great. Nope, still not enough, back again. Then, when I think we're done he tells me I can't throw it forward any more. I can only push it from the end closest to me. At this point I do swear. This thing is bloody heavy and barely moves at all using this move.

Just when I think the embarrassment is over he wants me to lie on my back and lift my torso and legs at the same time.

"Just a small lift." he commands. It's a good job this is Tiny and I adore him, or he'd be getting a fat lip around now. "Crunch up and imagine I'm there between your trembling thighs, making you wet... Now push up harder..." To that he smirks at my face, which is showing complete shock. I've probably turned an interesting shade of puce as well.

I manage to lift my torso less than inch. Tiny fails to look impressed. "I know you can do it harder, your eyes tell me more! ... Your sweat makes me proud of you, which means you want it as much as me." That's too much for me and I pull myself to a seated position and burst into giggles. If this had been in any other context, such as one of the books I love to read, it would have been a bloody hot scene. As it is, I'm a sweaty mess sitting on a gym mat, too exhausted to try anymore.

"What's with you?" Tiny asks. He's really confused and has no idea how his innocent words just affected me. Damn this sexual frustration I'm suffering thanks to Alex.

"I'm sorry. I've just not got it in me today." I mumble. "Why don't you go do your session and I'll go cool down on the cross trainer and grab a shower. I'll meet you in the coffee bar when you're done." I don't wait for his answer, instead I stand and grab my gym towel and water bottle before heading over to the cross trainer to finish off.

I'm not sure how I'm going to handle another seven weeks of this. Granted the guys aren't what I'd expected. They're certainly brawny but they're not as brainless as I'd given them credit for. In just a few days they've started to feel like family. I can't let some silly emotions and fantasies get in the way here. I'm supposed to be working and acting like a professional after all.

I push myself harder than I should on the cross trainer, it's supposed to be a cool down after all, but I need to punish myself somehow and this is the only way I can think of to do it right now.

I hit the showers and stand there for ages under the lukewarm flow. What is it with gyms and cold showers? Do they think we're all getting sexually worked up out there and need to cool down our libidos? Whatever the reason, the shower works. I'm almost back to myself by the time I hit the coffee bar and slink into the softest, comfiest leather chair I can find whilst I wait for Tiny to join me.

CHAPTER THIRTEEN

Sally

I pull up my email on my phone while I'm waiting and almost spit my coffee across the room when I read the message from my boss. He can't do this to me! It was bad enough that I was landed with this lame ass assignment, but now he's gone too far. He's taken my story; the corrupt councilor and let that jerk Rob get hold of my research and run with it. And then. And then I can't believe what I'm reading, he wants me to do a fluff story whilst I'm on the road with the tour. This day just gets worse.

He wants me to log onto a dating site, a bloody free crappy dating site, and try and expose the married men who use it to cheat on their wives. Is he mad? He must be to think I'd lower myself like this. But of course, he's not mad. He's wily. The last line of the email reminds me how precarious my job is; how I need to be a team player right now, and write the titilating gossipy stuff that sells the paper. Stuff isn't a word I'd have chosen; crap fits the role much better.

He also had the cheek to ask me to use some decent pictures, one's where I'm wearing something nice and have my face on. That's the phrase he uses when he wants me to wear make-up at some dull social affair the management of the paper is hosting. Smile and look pretty. Ugh. The thought of this assignment makes me feel dirty before I've even started it.

In his defense the tour alone isn't making the best use of my time. I do have the capacity to work on a second story, but this? This is like some tacky MTV show.

I download the app he's mentioned and start thinking of what to put for my bio. I stick to the basics for now. When it asks what I'm looking for I give it some thought. I definitely don't want to scare them off by saying I'm looking for a long-term relationship, but at the same time I don't want to come across as easy. I choose 'want to date but nothing serious'. That should get rid of any one-night stand wannabes.

The questions I'm working through seem fairly straightforward, they're asking if I've got kids, smoke, have a car, my height. I pause at that one? Why height? Then I realize the last thing I'd want is to go out with someone shorter than me. I go through the rest of the bio, careful to make it as truthful as possible; yet just interesting enough I may get a bite. The more I think about it, this could be good for me. I've got a few friends who met their partner on a dating site and are still together. It beats having to go out clubbing and trawling the bars for someone as well. If nothing else it will help distract me from thoughts of Alex.

I'm trying to find a decent profile picture when I'm surprised by Tiny coming up behind me. "What are you up to?" he asks as he sees the photo on my phone. "Is that you? You look hot!" he compliments me. I guess I do feel good in this picture. It was taken before one of the boring work parties. I'd worn my slinky red dress, put some make up on and even straightened my hair for a change. I'd felt good that night.

I don't want Tiny to see what I'm doing, I'm ashamed to be working on this type of assignment, and I'd hate him to think I was on a dating site for real.

"Yep, thanks, are we going?" I mumble, quickly closing down the dating app and grabbing my bag. Tiny looks a little surprised by my haste to leave, especially considering I've barely touched my coffee. He knows how much I need my caffeine fix after the gym.

***

Back in the safety of my room I get my iPad out and open the dating site again. The first page that greets me is full of photos of men. The best way to describe it is somewhere between an embarrassing high school yearbook and a Crimewatch appeal by the police.

Where are all the hot, male bodies? This screen is full of dorks, thugs, overweight losers and more. I mentally reprimand myself for being so shallow. After all, an image doesn't tell me anything about their personality; or does it?

There's a guy posed in front of a helicopter and in a morning suit. I scroll through his other images. He's trying to tell a story here. He's at the races, in front of a flash car, on a tropical holiday. Yep, he's selling himself as wealthy. Nope, he's too much like a sugar daddy for me.

I haven't had time to fully complete my profile but the screen for 'My Matches' has a lot of results already. I scroll down slowly. There must be an error in the settings somewhere as its only showing older men. There's not one under forty. Okay, some of these are old enough to be my father. Yeuch.

As I read through some of the profiles I feel my heart soften a little. Some of these guys seem desperate to find the one. They're looking for marriage or long-term relationships. From the little I did enter on my profile it's obvious to me these aren't suitable matches for me, nor for my article.

There's a little icon at the top of the screen that catches my attention. It's got a number three in it. I click on it and find I have three messages already. This should be interesting.

That red dress would look better on my bedroom floor.

Okay, I wasn't expecting that. I quickly find the delete conversation button.

Hi sweetie, how are you? You seem very nice.

That's not so bad I guess but how can he make that judgment based on one photo and a couple of lines about me?

Hi, may I start off by saying you look like a very attractive lady who has a beautiful smile and stunning eyes to match. I am looking for that Special Lady if she exists who is sadly missing from my life. Someone who is kind, honest, trustworthy, fun to be with yet very caring and loving at the same time just like me. Would love to hear back from you?

xxx

Well that one makes me feel like a sleaze. The poor guy is just looking for love. I look at his profile photo; it's just so ordinary. When I scroll down his profile we have nothing in common. I feel sorry for him; I hope he finds what he's looking for. I send him a polite reply back to let him know I'm not the one.

I decide to fill my bio out a little, and add a couple more photos. Some of the guys on here don't even have one profile pic. How do they expect anyone to talk to them?

As I'm slowly scrolling through the pictures that are showing I think how weird it would be if someone I knew were on there. I understand that some people use this particular site just to set up one night stands and liaisons, but the majority seems to be looking for something a little more permanent.

I'm not sure I'm comfortable with how close to my home address some of these people are, it tells me that there are at least two guys who live within five hundred yards of my home postal code. That's a little creepy for me.

I scroll a little further down the page then pause. Shit. It happened. I look at the photo again to double check, it's him alright. I can't believe it. There on the bottom of the page. I know him. It's my friend's husband. And as far as I knew, when I spoke to her last week, she was under the impression they were still very much happily married.

I'm startled from my reverie when I hear Tiny knocking on my door, reminding me it's time to check out and head over to the next venue.

I close the offending page on my iPad and shove it in my bag. What should I do? What can I do? Right now, I feel like my world is upside down. How do you even begin to tell a friend that she's living a lie?

I don't have time to figure it out right now; we've got to go. I grab my bags and head down to the minibus.

CHAPTER FOURTEEN

Sally

Tonight's theater is one of the smallest on the tour according to Eric. There are fewer than 700 seats, but it's sold out which is good. It does mean though the guys need to rehearse to ensure they can fit the routines on to the stage safely.

I'm watching from the wings as they perform their Officer and a Gentleman routine. They all look hot in their white uniforms and caps. I'd expected them to go with something soft for this routine, but no, they've gone for 'Sexy and I know it' by LMFAO. I love the beat to this song.

They march out to the stage in time with the intro beat, pause then tilt their caps at the audience. Because it's a rehearsal I'm saved the ear-piercing shriek I know that will attract, but I can still hear it in my head. All six of the dancers are in this routine as it's just after the interval.

They click their fingers along to the music, at the same time moving their feet incredibly quickly and agilely in the steps from the music video.

There's a lot of hip grinding in this routine, and that combined with just the appearance of the white suits is hot. The white jackets have the illusion of polished gold buttons but I know that underneath it's Velcro that's keeping them fastened, allowing them to supposedly undo one button at a time without fumbling. At the first 'I'm Sexy and I know it' chorus the jackets are gone; leaving glistening toned abs in their place. Chest muscles flex at the 'look at that body' lines in the song.

Just before the wiggle, wiggle, wiggle they reach down in unison, grabbing hold of their waistbands. In one flick of the wrist their trousers are gone. Every time the song says wiggle, boy do they wiggle. Their hands either side of their heads, their hips pushing back and forwards so fluidly. In those tight little dark briefs it's easy to see who's well packed and who isn't. The audience doesn't seem to care. They scream regardless.

At the final 'I'm Sexy and I know it' Jackal does a standing back flip, landing perfectly into a split. Bloody hell, these guys really are fit!

The next routine is the cowboy routine. It's just Guido and Jonny. They perform this to Five Finger Death Punch's 'Bad Company'. It's slow to open, allowing them to stroll languidly onto the stage. Dark blue denim jeans, colorful checkered shirts, and cowboy hats pulled low over their foreheads.

They use the toy gun in their hands to push up the brim of the hats, revealing cheeky grins and sparkling eyes. The guns are tucked into the back of the waistbands and their thumbs hook into the belt loops as they strut around the stage, postulating and gesturing at each other.

At the chorus 'Bad Company' they start to flip across the stage in opposite directions. It's absolutely awesome to watch, even with their clothes on. This routine is one where they only take their shirts off. It's more about their agility on the stage. The sex comes from the moves. The thrusts. The grinds. The twists. The lights showcasing their highly toned, very well oiled, backs and chests. You can see the power in these naked torsos. Even watching from the wings I can feel it.

At one point Guido slides across the stage on his knees. Now I get why they wear those very unsexy black kneepads.

As the song slows towards the end they face off against each other, assuming the position of a stand off. There's a flash of light at the final 'Until the Day I die' and Guido remains standing – the victor, Jonny lying crumpled on the floor. The lights fade out.

I prefer watching the rehearsals to the live shows. I still get to experience the lighting, the loud music and the sexy atmosphere. I just get to appreciate it without the heckling and cat calling. I'm seriously ashamed to be female when it comes to some of the fans.

***

Rehearsal finished early enough that I've got time to take a stroll down the beachfront before we grab an early dinner. It's a long time since I came to Bridlington. It's not the classiest of places, just one step up really from Blackpool in terms of the people who tend to come here; but I have good childhood memories of visiting here.

I managed to sneak out while everyone was getting changed. The contrast between the quiet beachfront and the bustle backstage at the theater is massive. There seems to be an army of unpaid volunteers at each of the theaters we attend. The dressers are the most fun, over the years they've seen it all and heard it all and as shy as I am, I feel most comfortable around them.

One of them today expressed surprise that the guys were so normal, and had very few demands. It's only when someone calls it to attention that I realize they're right. A lot of touring groups demand all sorts of perks and privileges. Not my boys. I stop myself, less than a week on the road with them and I'm already calling them my boys. I guess I do feel protective of them.

She was telling me about the last group of strippers they'd had here. They'd demanded waist height mirrors so they could check out how their cocks looked, stuffed into their tiny briefs. She'd laughed hysterically when she told me how she'd walked in on them one day to discover their briefs weren't the only things that were tiny.

"And they use elastic bands to make their thingies look bigger." She'd shrieked with laughter. I'm way too innocent, as it took a few moments and several hand gestures for me to comprehend what she was saying. Ouch. That's got to hurt.

I walk back towards the theater, past a row of shops selling cheap, tacky souvenirs and spot the racks of loom bands on display. Everywhere I turn these days there's a rack of loom bands. Suddenly, my mind connects loom bands and elastic bands and I realize I'll never be able to walk past such a display again without blushing.

CHAPTER FIFTEEN

Sally

There's a meet and greet after the show tonight in the lobby of the theater. It's the first one I'm attending, although I believe they do them as often as they can. It's an opportunity to sell extra merchandise after all.

I know from the research I've done that some male strippers sell posters, and if you've purchased a poster then you can get on stage and meet them. Yep, they're not selling posters; they're effectively selling gropes! Eric doesn't operate that way. He's trying to keep the show hot, yet classy, to objectify the guys as little as possible, which isn't easy in this industry. Eric used to be a stripper in a past life as he calls it. His ideal is to take the good parts of that and use them for the Naked Night's and to steer clear of the more negative aspects he experienced.

The lobby is pulsating with bodies when I arrive and I'm quickly elbowed and shoved to the sidelines as a hen party arrives. I cringe inwardly at the sight. I'm not a snob, but hen parties are one of my pet hates. Normally sane women acting like sex-starved heathens for a night, getting high on alcohol.

"Go on Trudy, you know you wanna play with the boys." One of the women is pushed forward; it's the hen. She's wearing a nun's outfit with fake boobs, a sash and a tiara. God I want to throw up at the sight of it. The habit is so short her arse is practically on display.

"Show em your boobs Trudy," catcalls another of the hen party.

I catch Alex's expression and smile. I don't think anyone else saw it, it was so brief after all, but the look of disdain that just crossed his face was a picture. Of course Guido looks like all his Christmases have come at once. That man is such a whore.

"If you don't want em I'll have em love. I always said God made me chunky for a reason, because if I was thin I'd be a bad ass stripper!" She's obviously called Donna as I overhear her more sober friend chastise her.

"Ladies, ladies…" soothes Eric. "Calm down; there's plenty of time for you all to get to say hello." A small cheer goes up from the assembled rabble. Eric tries to get them to form some sort of line, rather unsuccessfully in my opinion, but it's a little more organized than it was before.

He's not daft as the merchandise table stands between the crowd and the Naked Night's who are lined up at the bottom of the room. I notice Alex and Tiny exchange a look; I recognize their code by now, they're checking out the exits just in case they get mobbed.

The girls on the table are exchanging money for calendars and photographs quicker than I can keep track. The steady stream of girls passes down the line of Naked Night's, some getting photos signed, others asking for pictures.

I'm shocked when one girl approaches Guido and pulls down her dress to expose her breast and nipple. "Can you sign my boob for me Guido." She simpers. "I bloody love you!" Guido smirks and takes the pen from her hand.

"Who do I sign it to?" He queries.

"I'm Lisa." She licks her lips, there's nothing erotic about the way she does it though. It's sleazy. "I've got somewhere else you can sign if you like love, but I can't show it out here." She sniggers. A silent exchange takes place between them. Well that's Guido sorted for the next five minutes after the show. I wonder how Lisa will react when she realizes he's all talk and no substance, if she'll be quite as vocal as plastic Barbie the other night.

Someone in the queue behind her makes a comment I can't hear and Lisa suddenly turns on them. "Why? 'Cause I'm fucking awesome love, and let's face it, who wouldn't want to be in my knickers." She boldly states. Well, I wouldn't for one. One of her friends tries to hurry her up, eager to get her own autograph I suspect.

"Feck off Danni; this one's mine." She leers at Guido who is grinning even more widely now. "Unless you fancy a threesome love?" Guido's face lights up even more. Great, now we'll have two disgruntled fans to deal with.

"How about a foursome?" another girl screams.

"What's your name love?" Guido is still grinning.

"I'm Amy. And trust me lover, when I touch you, you'll tremble all over." She promises.

If I listen to anymore of this I'll be breaking out into laughter. My initial disgust has been replaced by a hysterical need to laugh. These women are debasing themselves. I know some alcohol is involved, but still. Do they speak like this normally? Would they talk to their mothers with those mouths?

I can't get over how over exaggerated the whole thing feels and looks. It's like a hen party on crack. Oh hang on; this IS a hen party! I look for a way out. If I stay here much longer I'm afraid I'll catch something from this lot, and it won't be a sense of decorum that's for sure.

Spotting a fire exit I sneak outside, inhaling a breath of clean, fresh sea air. That's better. I walk over to the sea wall, sinking down slowly. Right now I can't decide if I'm loving this job or not. I feel cheap and dirty reporting anything that encourages this sort of behavior. How do I report on it without my personal distaste showing through the whole article? I've been taught to write from a distance, objectively. I'm finding it very hard to be objective here.

There's a thud as the fire exit door opens and closes. I look up to see Alex walking towards me. Damn. He's one of the reasons I'm finding it so hard to remain objective.

CHAPTER SIXTEEN

Sally

Last night I'd been so conscious of how close Alex was sitting next to me on the wall. It must have shown as he asked me what was wrong. I used the excuse of being worried about my friend. Alex pushed for more so I told him about the article I'd been asked to write and how I'd come across Gary on the dating site.

Alex had a funny look on his face when I mentioned the dating site. I can only assume he was considering checking it out as I know it helps men connect with other men as well as women.

Alex and I threw around some ideas, but what it all boiled down to was that if I was a true friend I had to say something. I couldn't keep quiet. As much as speaking up now would hurt Ashley, not speaking up would hurt more in the long run.

"Look at it this way." Alex offered. "If it was you, would you want to know?" He's right. As bad as finding out I'd been betrayed would be, not being told it was happening by a friend in the know would piss me off.

I'm still mulling this over as we board the minibus for the journey to the next theater.

The driver, Dan, told me we'll be on the road for a good hour and a half, more depending on traffic so I pull out my Kindle to read the latest Lili St Germain. I love her Seven Sons series, and the latest installment has just come out. I can lose myself in murder and revenge and not worry about my own problems for a while.

I'm totally engrossed in a scene where Sammi is in a dungeon being tortured yet again by Dornan when I feel something warm and heavy on my foot. I'm confused. I lower my Kindle to the empty seat at the side of me before looking down.

What I see causes the breath to leave my body. I want to scream. I REALLY want to scream but my mouth is moving and nothing but quiet whimpers are coming out.

I'm frozen to my seat so I can't even gesture for anyone to come and help me.

Jonny must have heard me whimpering as he gets out of his seat and comes to investigate.

"You okay Sally?" the last part of my name is cut off as he lets out a piercing scream. I'm amazed Dan didn't crash the minibus! He just looks at us all in the rear view mirror before asking if everyone's okay. I guess he's had worse happen to him than this when he's driving.

Jonny's scream has now alerted the others that something's wrong and there's a sudden rush of bodies at the side of me.

"What the fuck!" Tiny shouts. I'm not sure if I've heard him swear before, he's normally so well mannered around me.

I still can't get the words out, but my hands are now free and I point down at my foot where the terror lies.

Jonny is still screeching like a girl, quite funny considering I'm the girl and I can't actually get any noise from my strangled throat.

"Oh shit, I'm so sorry." Jackal says, he's holding an empty black canvas holdall in his hand and looking very pale.

I look from the holdall to the floor, and back to the holdall. He's got to be joking me.

There on the floor, laid over my foot is a snake. Despite what I imagined, the body where it lies on my foot is warm. I'd expected it to be a cold, scaly creature and always shied away from them. That's right. I'm terrified of snakes.

"Where the bloody hell has that come from and what's it doing here?" Eric sounds furious, his anger solely directed at Jackal.

"It's a Royal Python, I got it off a man in a pub last night." Eric's glare is causing the normally calm Jackal to stumble with his words.

"I didn't ask what it was." Eric shouts. "What's it doing here?"
"I thought I could use it in the act." Jackal offers, he sounds like a chastised child; his head low to his body as he answers.

"How the fuck did you think we'd work a snake into the act?" Eric mutters. "You do know how much hassle the theaters would give us, not to mention the bloody councils. You have to have a separate dressing room and attendant for a fucking dog in a show, god knows what hoops we'd have to go through with a fucking snake you idiot!" Eric is now going slightly red in the face. Jackal meanwhile is whiter than ever. Jonny is as far back in the bus as he can get from both the snake and me. If I weren't so scared this would be funny.

"Excuse me?" my voice is still barely a whisper as I point at the snake still lying over my foot. "Help?"

"Here give me that bag." Tiny reaches for it, looking inside, then turns to Jackal, perplexed. "Where's the bedding?"

"What?" Jackal hasn't a clue what Tiny is talking about, from the look of the faces around us, no one else has either.

"You've got a Royal Python and you didn't think to ask how to look after it?" Tiny looks disgusted. "Pass me some newspapers, now!" he ends on a shout, as Jackal obviously didn't move quickly enough for him.

"Listen Sally, it's going to be okay. My uncle used to have one of these. Let me just sort this bag out and I'll lift it off you. I know it doesn't help but right now she's probably more scared of you than you are of her." He reassures. Yeah. Right. I highly doubt it.

"They like the dark, and the warmth." He continues. "She probably got out of the bag because this idiot didn't add any bedding and followed the warmth of the exhaust along the bus. We just need to get some bedding in the bag for her and I'll put her back." He turns to Alex who's standing just behind him. "Can you check on the internet and see if there are any reptile shops in Grimsby, I think there is one there from memory. We need to find somewhere to take her."

Jackal starts to protest, muttering about how much money he paid for the snake last night but Tiny interrupts him.

"Don't be so bloody stupid Jackal. I thought you were afraid of snakes as well as this idiot here." He gestures to Jonny who's still hiding. "This poor thing doesn't need to be with someone who doesn't have a clue how to take care of it. We're not a bloody circus act!" His tone is full of disgust.

By this point Eric and Guido have filled the bag with shredded newspaper. Tiny reaches over carefully, talking to me the whole time.

"Right Sally, I'm going to gently lift her away from you. I'm going to move slowly so I don't startle her, okay?" I nod my head. As he lifts the snake I start to shiver. I'd only seen a part of her body and her head, but what he reveals makes me feel almost sick. She's almost four foot in length. He raises her gently, almost reverently, and places her in the bag. Once he's secured the bag he passes it back to Jackal. "Go sit down and make sure that bag stays closed." Tiny instructs. Jackal takes the bag, almost reluctantly and moves towards the back of the minibus. As soon as he's sat down Jonny shoots to the seat in front of mine. He's still looking quite grey.

Alex and Tiny confer for a few moments before Alex moves to the front of the bus to talk to Dan, the driver.

"It's okay Sally, we're going to make a quick detour and drop her off at the reptile store in Grimsby." He reassures me as he takes the seat at the side of me, careful to move my Kindle out of the way before he sits down. "Are you okay?" I almost cry at the concern in his voice. I love this guy; he's such a gentle giant.

"I'll be fine." My voice is slowly returning, but the shaking in my hands is still there. Tiny sees me looking at my hands and takes one in his.

"Of course you'll be fine. You're stronger than you think lovely girl." He smiles at me. I love his smile. He sits beside me the rest of the way to the shop. He's the one who takes the snake into the reptile store.

There's a huge sigh of relief from everyone on the minibus when he returns empty handed.

"Hope you got my money back." Jackal mutters. He's soon silenced by the look Tiny gives him in return.

"Jackal, sit down and shut up before I punch your bloody lights out for what you did to Sally." Tiny roars. Jackal's just about to protest when he sees the look on Tiny's face. He sits down and shuts up.

The minibus pulls up outside yet another Travelodge, and I give a silent cheer. I can't wait to get in the shower and scrub the feeling of snake off me. It doesn't matter that she's no longer on the bus, it's like I can still feel the ghost of her on me. I'm almost rude in the way I snatch the key from the receptionist and rush to the room.

As soon as I enter I throw my bags to the floor, switch the shower on and tear my clothes off. It's only now the delayed shock hits me and I fall to a heap in the bottom of the shower, huge sobs racking my body. The water rains down on me, slowly warming the chill from my body.

Well, one thing I can say for this particular assignment. It's never boring!

CHAPTER SEVENTEEN

Alex

Sally shot off like a rocket once she'd got her room key. I know the experience on the bus must have scared her, but I don't think any of us realized quite how badly.

Eric is still giving Jackal a hard time over it. It was a stupid move to make, especially as he's not too fond of snakes himself. He's a good bloke but sometimes he just doesn't think.

I took note of Sally's room number; my room is only a few doors away from her. I unpack a few items, not much as again we're only here for the one night, and decide to go see if she's okay.

Her door isn't properly latched, anyone walking past wouldn't have noticed, but as I knock it slowly edges open. I can hear the shower running. I don't want to disturb her and am about to walk away when I hear the sobs. Christ, they sound awful.

"Sally?" I call out. She doesn't seem able to hear me over the sound of her crying and the heavy jet of water coming from the showerhead. I'm not sure how long she's been in there but the small bathroom is full of steam. I call again, a little louder. She must hear me as her sobs stop with a stutter.

"Who's there?" I've scared her, there's a fearful tremble in her voice.

"It's just Alex, I wanted to make sure you were okay after what happened on the minibus. The door wasn't shut properly."

The steam is slowly fading as she's shut the shower off to hear me. I can't see much through the misted up glass, but what I can see causes an erection to tent my workout pants. Sally's got curves in all the right places.

"I, I'm fine." She stutters out. "Please leave." There's still a tremble in her voice. I just want to draw her into my arms and hold her there safe.

"Why don't I just wait out in the bedroom, give you a moment. I need to make sure you're okay. You scared me just now with all that crying." I suggest.

"You're not going to go away are you?" I hear a little bit of Sally's stubborn attitude in that question. I smile.

"Nope."

"Fine." She huffs. "Give me a minute."

I walk back out to the bedroom to wait for her. Her clothes she was wearing are strewn all over the floor. Unless she took some fresh ones into the bathroom with her that means she's only going to be wearing a towel. Shit. No way I can talk my erection away if that happens. I sit on the bed against the headboard, pulling a pillow over my lap to hide my predicament.

Moments later Sally emerges from the bathroom, a slightly less than adequate towel wrapped around her. She has great legs. I follow the view up, pausing on the rise and fall of her breasts as they peep out over the top of the towel, slightly more than a handful there, and reluctantly move my eyes higher to her face.

Her dark hair hangs in wet strands around her face. She shrugs her shoulders at me in defeat as I gesture for her to come sit beside me on the bed. She moves towards me though.

She leaves a large gap between us until she sees the look I give her. I wrap my arm around her shoulder and she moves over to lean into me. She fits perfectly, like she was made for me. She lowers her head to my shoulder and I gently stroke her damp hair.

"Was it that bad?" I ask. Her only reply is a small movement of her head. She's crying again, this time silently. A tear rolls from her face, dampening my white t-shirt. I can't stand to see her hurting like this.

"You're that afraid of snakes?" A small nod again. I lift her chin with my finger, bringing her eyes level with mine and wipe away the tear that's forming. "Then you are the bravest person I know." I smile at her. "Look at how Jonny reacted. Like a big girls blouse." I chuckle. She tries to smile, but she's still struggling. I look over to the dressing table where the obligatory tiny kettle and coffee sachets sit. "You want a coffee?" I gesture. She looks over to follow my eye line and shakes her head.

"Don't go." She whispers. She's not really holding me, more leaning on me, but as she utters the words the space between us diminishes. I tighten my arm around her shoulder a little more and I'm sure I hear her sigh.

We must sit like that for a good hour, no words being spoken. Slowly Sally comes back to herself, until she realizes that she's laid on a bed with me in just a towel. A towel that has risen to only just cover the magnificence that is her arse; and is revealing a hell of a lot of toned thigh right now. She moves suddenly, too suddenly for her as the towel falls and exposes her breasts. Fuck. I almost come in my pants at the view before me. I want to reach out, to touch, and to caress. I can't. She's not aware of how I feel about her. I don't want to scare her, especially after what she's just been through.

Sally grabs the towel and hurries from the bed like a startled rabbit. She grabs one of her bags and runs for the bathroom, slamming and locking the door behind her this time. No words are spoken, but her face was bright red.

To say the moment was lost is a bit of an understatement.

Lying on that bed, holding Sally in my arms, felt so comfortable and right. Despite my dick constantly distracting me, I was happy just to lie there.

I don't know how I'm going to do it but I want Sally. Not in the one night stand way most of the guys want a woman. I want her as a friend, a companion and fuck yes as a lover.

"You okay?" I shout through the thick wooden door.

"I, I'm fine." She doesn't quite sound it, but I'm not going to push it right now.

"I'll let you get dressed, give you some space." I offer. "Why don't you come down to the bar when you're done and I'll buy you a stiff drink. I think you've earned it don't you?"

"Thanks." I hear through the door, I'm pretty sure I can hear some muttered curse words in the background as well. "I'll see you down there. Give me half an hour to sort my hair?" She asks.

"Sure. Take your time." I leave the room making damned sure the door is locked behind me this time. I sure as hell don't want anyone else wandering in and seeing her in her underwear

CHAPTER EIGHTEEN

Sally

What the hell just happened? I ask myself. I spent the last hour or so laying on a bed with Alex, he was fully clothed whilst I was wearing a towel that was barely there. The worst part is how good it felt. And it sure didn't feel like my brother was hugging me. That has to be the most sensual hug I've ever had. You know what? That's the BEST hug I've ever had. I realize this is what was missing from my previous relationships. Feeling close with each other; yet no expectations of sex at the end of it.

My pussy is complaining that there was no sex though. How can he be gay? It's such a bloody waste. I'm frustrated as hell, but I'm no longer scared. Alex has a way about him that seems to calm me. Perhaps it is just that he's gay, there's no pressure there on me. I know I'm not being looked at like a potential bed partner, just as a friend. It's why I get on so well with Tiny as well. He's so happily taken with his fiancée that I feel safe with him. They're both good guys. Hot as hell, but still good guys.

It's quite flattering to my ego to be seen walking around with these two The looks of envy and jealousy cast my way make me laugh. If only these women knew the truth. That said the looks of lust and lasciviousness that I often see get my hackles up. I'm protective of my buddies.

"Get over yourself Sally Evans." I tell my reflection in the mirror. "He's gay. He's not going to go straight for you, so just get over it." Besides, what the hell would a hot guy like him see in a girl like me?

I take stock of my body, there's no full length mirror in the bathroom but what I can see shows me overfull breasts, a curvaceous arse and heavy legs. I'm no Barbie doll that's for sure. I'm not fat, but I'm not thin. I guess I'm more athletic than anything.

My hair looks like a tangled mess. I plug in the straighteners deciding I can't go downstairs looking like this. I can't remember the last time I got them out; I'm not a girly girl at all. I don't primp and preen. I tend to just throw my hair in a ponytail when it's wet from the shower. But even a ponytail wouldn't make this tangle look better.

I'm wearing my comfy jeans and a loose white shirt that ties at the bottom. It's become a sort of uniform for me, and it helps put me in work mode. When I'm in my work zone frame of mind nothing gets to me. It's like a barrier between the rest of the world and me. It helps make me anonymous, and able to blend into the background. Right now I wish I could just disappear into the ground, never mind the background. I'm still pretty humiliated at what happened in front of Alex.

I shut the straightener off and head out of the room. I just hope that my stupid behavior hasn't ruined our friendship.

***

Alex is sitting with Tiny when I find them. They seem to prefer the comfy sofas and chairs scattered around, whilst the other guys are propping up the bar as usual.

"You okay Sally?" Tiny asks me. I panic, wondering if Alex has told him about finding me sobbing in the shower. A small flush of embarrassment is making its way up my chest as I look at Alex. He must sense what I'm thinking as he gives me a subtle shake of his head.

"I'm fine, just spooked me a bit." I reply. "I've got a morbid fear of snakes." I feel silly now. I'm a grown woman confessing a stupid phobia.

"Let me get you a drink, what do you want?" Tiny rises from his seat to head to the bar.

"Can I just have a black coffee please?" Right now I'd kill for a coffee.

"Sure hun. Take a seat and I'll bring it straight back. Alex?" He points to Alex's glass, which is still almost full, and Alex declines. "Back in a minute." With that he's gone. I find myself standing there, feeling gawky and awkward.

"Come on Sally, I don't bite, remember?" Alex smirks as he pats the seat next to him on the sofa. Cautiously I sit down. I'm careful to keep plenty of space between us. I'm about to ask Alex if he told Tiny when he beats me to it.

"I didn't say a word, nor will I. Don't worry." He gives me that panty-melting smile of his. My heart breaks a little more. No matter how much I want him, I can't have him.

"Thank you. I appreciate that more than you know." Alex reaches over and pats my knee reassuringly. Too quickly his hand has gone, leaving a burning sensation behind and my pussy yearning for his touch to return.

I'm screwed.

CHAPTER NINETEEN

Sally

The theater is packed tonight, this one has capacity for over a thousand I'm told but Eric has asked me to sit out front. He's saved me a seat on the front row. He wants me to experience this exactly like the audience does. I try and object, letting him know I watched the bike scene the other night from the back of the theater but he ignores me.

"That doesn't count Sally. Come on. If you're going to write about this then you need to experience it properly." He's right. I know he's right. But I'm really not the kind of girl you'd find front and center in the audience at one of these shows. Let's face it. I'm not the kind of girl you'd find in the audience anywhere.

The show takes on a different dimension watching from the audience. I understand now why Eric asked me to sit here. From the wings or the back of the auditorium it looks good, but from here it looks amazing.

The combination of the costumes, lighting and the sheer athletic ability of the guys all work to create an unbelievable tension in the audience. I may not respect these women I'm sitting amongst, but I've got to admit they're totally immersed in the experience.

I watch the routines with pride. I know how much work goes into each one just choreographing it to get it right. Each shimmy, slither, jerk and thrust is carefully placed in the routine. The hours in the gym as well as rehearsals mean that when I look at the stage I see not just six guys, but six hot as all hell guys.

I'm still struggling with the crude lust the audience projects. They don't see what I see. It's as though where I see six people; they see six slabs of meat or sex toys.

Sitting in the front row has exposed me to the worst of it. The girls who buy these tickets have one thing on their mind. Getting on the stage and groping and manhandling the talent. They have no interest in the person on stage, just the body and the bragging rights that fucking them would give them. If I last a full performance sat next to them I'll definitely need to scrub myself clean in the shower. I feel sullied just sitting in close proximity to them.

It's time for one of Alex's solos whilst the guys do a more complicated costume change. I'm amazed at how clinical the whole costume experience is. Each guy has a volunteer dresser backstage, and a rack of clothes arranged in the order of the routines. Despite most of them being Velcro fastenings they often have only moments to swap outfits so it's timed down to the minute.

The single chair is brought front and center to the stage and I suddenly wish I wasn't sitting here. In this routine Alex chooses a member of the audience and pretty much gives her a private lap dance. I don't want to watch this up close and personal. I realize that this emotion cascading through me is jealousy. I've never felt jealous before with my previous partners, so why the hell do I feel it now when Alex isn't even mine? Alex can't be mine.

Before he leaves the stage to come into the audience Alex seeks me out with his eyes. I give him a look of warning. No. He wouldn't!

Alex stalks over to me, and offers me his hand. I don't have a choice other than to accept. Deep down my inner voice is yelling 'Hell, yeah. You go for it girl.' I don't want to be on a stage, publicly humiliated in front of these harpies. But part of me, that deep inner part of me, can't refuse the opportunity of being this close to Alex. Yes, it's an act. It's make-believe. But for five minutes I can pretend that it's just him and me. I can be selfish and take this experience, file it away in my memory treasure box, and bring it out on nights when I'm cold and lonely.

The blindfold has altered my senses. I'm especially aware of Alex's presence. It's a heightened awareness. Alex doesn't quite follow his usual routine. Some nights he offers slightly less, it depends on how 'grabby' the woman he has picked is. Tonight, he guides my hand to his belt buckle, allowing me to release it. I draw the belt out, slowly as I've watched him do in his routines. Now he draws my hand back to the button on his jeans. I draw in a breath. He's never done this whilst I've been watching. He draws one of my hands into his waistband and uses the other to release his zipper. Has the temperature in here suddenly gone up? I'm burning up here.

I can feel the length of him through his boxers. He uses my hand to caress it. Fuck, this is so erotic. I'm so turned on right now I'm pretty sure my knickers are drenched. All I'm aware of right now is the feel of Alex in my hand. I've totally zoned out the noise from the audience. Right now, blinded by the darkness I can believe that this is just he and I. I tighten my grip slightly. I can't help it.

Alex moves away quickly, startling me. Shit. I went too far. The noise from the auditorium seeps back into my consciousness, reminding me where I am. I'm ashamed.

I can feel Alex moving back towards me. I'd swear he's a whisper away from my lips. I want so much to just move my head slightly forward and caress his hardness with my mouth, but what if I'm wrong. How stupid would I look if he weren't there? I'd probably fall flat on my bloody face.

From the sound of the screaming I'm guessing we've hit the point where he's dropped his boxer briefs. Shit, the thought of Alex naked behind that towel has me shifting uncomfortably on my seat. I can feel how drenched my knickers are.

Oh. My. God. Alex has taken one of my hands and placed it on his towel-clad cock. I can't help it; involuntarily I draw my hand back as if I've burned it. The noise in the auditorium is at deafening levels now. Suddenly I can see again. I can't quite focus though as there's a spotlight aimed right at me. I look at the view in front of me and can't help the laughter that bursts out. I know the routine, it shouldn't have come as a surprise to me, but the sight of Alex's union jack clad cock just a breath away from my face was too much.

Alex gets a standing ovation. Little does he know he got one from my pussy as well. As he guides me back to the audience the questions from the over eager fans begin, assaulting my senses. I give Alex my best glare. It's what he'd expect from me after all. Deep down though, I can't be angry with him. That was the most sensual, erotic experience I've ever had. My heart wilts a little at the thought it might be the only one I ever get.

CHAPTER TWENTY

Sally

As soon as I sat down the heckling and cackling started either side of me. The volume and the words were too much and I made a hasty escape, desperate for fresh air.

Eric found me outside the stage door, a concerned look on his face.

"You alright, Sally? He's an idiot, he shouldn't have done that and picked on you. When I wanted you to experience the show I didn't mean from on stage."

"It's fine Eric, don't worry. It was certainly an experience. I've just got a stinking headache. I think today was just a bit much for me. I think I'll head back to the hotel if you don't mind. See you in the morning."

Before he can protest I've turned and am striding away. The cool night air is doing a fairly good job of cooling down my overheated skin, but not my libido.

I have got a headache; that much is true. It wasn't the fiasco on the bus with the snake that brought it on though. It was being on stage with Alex, wanting him, and all the while knowing I can't have him.

Alex

I glance out from the stage and see that Sally's seat is empty. She hasn't returned from the interval. Shit. I guess that means I'm in big trouble.

I struggle to concentrate for the rest of the show, but I don't let it affect my performance.

During a costume change Eric tells me that Sally went back to the hotel as she was complaining of a headache. He may believe that, especially after the stress from earlier, but I don't. This is my fault. I've pissed her off.

As soon as I can, I escape the theater and head back to the hotel. There's no sign of Sally in the bar so I go knock on her door.

"Who is it?" comes the muffled response.

"It's Alex. I wanted to make sure you were okay?" I ask.

The door cracks open slightly, but she's got the chain on so I can't go any further than the hallway.

"I'm fine. I've just got a stinking headache and need an early night." I can hear the pain in her voice, and her face is deathly pale. Maybe she has got a headache after all.

"You need any tablets or anything?" I offer.

"No thanks, I've had some. I'll be fine once I've had some sleep."

"Look, Sally..." I pause, unsure how to word what I want to say, but she stops me anyway.

"Look Alex, it's fine. The stage thing was fine. I'm not angry if that's what's bothering you. I just don't feel very well right now, so if you'll excuse me I'm going back to bed." She's about to close the door on me.

"Sally." She looks up at me. "I'm sorry. I shouldn't have done it. Sleep well." I turn and walk away to my room. I don't want to walk away though. I want to bust down that door and pull her into my arms, even if it is just to hold her close all night whilst she sleeps.

I hope I haven't ruined our friendship.

Sally

Damn Alex for knocking on my door. This isn't fair. He has no clue how just the sight of him affects me.

As if I haven't got enough problems right now. Between worrying about whether I'll have a job at the end of this assignment, and how to tell my friend her husband is probably cheating on her I am beyond stressed.

I look back at the iPad, which is lying innocently on the bed. The dating app is open and the screen is showing Gary's dating profile. He say's he's single and has no kids. The lying shit. Is that what this is about? He feels emasculated because they've got a baby now?

Ashley is one of the nicest girls you could meet. She's attractive, funny and just good to be around. I know she didn't have the easiest pregnancy, and did gain some weight but when I saw her the other week she looked great.

I'm screwed at the moment, as this really isn't the sort of news you can give someone over the phone. It needs to be done face to face. That means I have to wait around another seven weeks for the tour to finish before I can meet up with her. Seven weeks is far too long. I dread to think of the damage that could be done to their marriage in that time.

Perhaps there's some innocent explanation for Gary being on the site. After all I'm not on there to date. Yeah. Right. Keep telling yourself that Sally, they'll put you in the nuthouse.

There's nothing else for it, I click on the message icon on Gary's profile and start to type:

Hi Gary

Fancy seeing you on here! I didn't realize that you and Ashley had split up. I'm so sorry to hear that. Hope you're well.

S

xxx

Hopefully that's innocent enough and shouldn't startle him. I'm about to shut down the app when I notice I have several incoming messages. I open them up and groan. More losers. The last message shocks me though. It's so graphic in it's intent I require mind bleach to erase it. Yeuch. I can't log out and shut down the iPad quickly enough.

I close my eyes, but the content of that message plays on my mind. This time though, it's not the creep from the dating site but Alex that is suggesting erotic acts. With that thought on my mind I fall into a blissful sleep.

CHAPTER TWENTY ONE

Sally

Breakfast was going okay until Tiny suggested he, Alex and I should hit the gym again before we leave.

"I've only just recovered from the last session." I whine. I'm not lying. I feel like an old woman twice my age after going to the gym with these two.

"I'll take it easy on you I promise." Tiny smirks. Like I believe that.

"This one's got a hot tub." Alex offers. That seals the deal. They can go workout and I'll soak my aching limbs in the hot tub. Tiny obviously realizes my intent though.

"No workout, no hot tub baby girl." He smirks. I'd love to wipe that smirk off his face right now. As though the bloody man can read my mind he continues. "I want to teach you some boxing moves today, they're great for toning your arms and general cardio fitness."

"So I get to punch you?" I ask.

"Well, you get to punch the pads I'm holding up for you." He offers. That's good enough for me. Sounds like a perfect way to release some of this tension.

"Now that I'd like to see." Alex laughs.

***

The gym is quiet when we get there for which I'm grateful. I'm even more grateful when Tiny pulls us over to a secluded corner out of sight of the other gym members.

He's made me do the usual warm up on the treadmill and the silly active cardio stretches. I feel like a fool swinging my arms here and there and kicking my legs out in exaggerated steps but he knows what he's doing.

He passes me a pair of boxing gloves to wear. They feel odd, not heavy, more off balance. He holds a couple of pads in front of his face. When I look at them they resemble faces. Now this I could have fun with.

"I want you to punch into each of the pads, your left hand into the right one and vice versa. I'll keep count. Hit it with everything you've got."

He corrects the angle of my hand after the first couple of hits, after that I'm in the zone. The pads take on the faces of my boss Fred, and my friend's husband Gary. I hit them with everything I've got.

"Slow down girl, you've got a few more repetitions of these to go yet." Tiny advises. Oops. I may have been a tad overenthusiastic.

This is a lot more interesting than the viper crawl he had me doing last time, and a hell of a lot more fun.

After a short break he asks me to jab upwards this time, my hands and arms at a slightly different angle. I think he calls this an upper cut.

I enjoy the boxing element of the routine but after that he has me doing burpees. I ask you. Does he go out of his way to find embarrassing positions to put me in? I make the mistake of asking him.

"Well, now that you mention it, your arse does look great when it's up in the air like that." He smirks. Lucky for him I'm stuck in this hands down, arse in the air position or I'd have slapped him for that. The grin on his face tells me he knows.

When I've completed the humiliation that is burpees he gets me to lift some light dumbbells. Again he corrects the angle of my arm. Apparently I'm working my shoulders instead of my chicken wings. As soon as he mentions chicken wings I pay attention. I recall a YouTube video a friend recently showed me of a 'Fat Granny Twerking'. She hadn't started twerking with her arse; she'd started twerking with the chicken wings on her arms. They flapped around all flabby and loose, it was gross. I'm paranoid that as I get older I'll end up looking like that so I pay close attention to what Tiny tells me for the rest of the session.

The hot tub is heaven. I'm glad I packed a swimsuit just in case we came across a pool on our travels. I hadn't expected to have company though so it doesn't cover as much as I'd have liked.

I exhale a gasp when Alex walks into the tub area. He's wearing black swimming trunks and they seem to draw the eye to that V of flesh that sits just above his waistband. Tiny follows close behind him, offering up a wolf whistle. "Damn, it should be against the law to look that hot in a bathing suit." He grins at me. I blush. I'm not used to compliments. I don't know about you but put downs seem much easier to believe and accept than compliments.

"Why thank you kind sir." Alex bows to Tiny and I can't help giggling. "Looking pretty hot yourself man." Alex winks at Tiny who suddenly looks unsettled and can't seem to wait to get into the tub with me.

"I was talking about you in case you're wondering." He whispers in my ear, before casting a nervous glance over at Alex.

I laugh even louder. I love being with these guys. They're good medicine.

CHAPTER TWENTY TWO

Sally

We're heading up to Newcastle today for a couple of days; night off tonight and the performance is tomorrow. Dan the driver advises we'll be on the road around three hours depending on traffic so get comfortable.

I like Newcastle, there's a lovely little tapas bar I went to with friends on my last visit and I think I'll see if I can persuade Alex and Tiny to pay it a visit.

I either need to find a launderette or go shopping for some new clothes. I'm tired of washing my gym kit out in the bath.

I open my iPad to start writing up this weeks article and see that I have new messages on the dating site. I'm not sure if I can be bothered to open them if I'm honest. I can't see how I can get an article out of this that will keep Fred happy, unless he let's me just write one about the culture we live in where people feel this is the only way they can meet a new partner. That might work if I can spin it right for him.

Sighing I click on the button to log in and open the messages. Why can't it just show me the bloody thing in the notification email and save me all this hassle.

As I expected there are several suggestive messages, mostly from men without profile pictures. I just delete those. There are also a couple of just happy to chat messages from some guys that I'll come back to later. The one that gets my heart racing is a message from Gary.

I open the message reluctantly.

If you want to do what's best for Ashley, you'll forget you saw me on here. We haven't split. Ashley's such a prude, as well you know. I just log on here occasionally for a little dirty talk, nothing else. I'm still happily married.
G

I can't tell the tone it was written in. That's the problem with the written word. Is it aggressive or am I just imagining it.

He's right. Ashley is the biggest prude I know. She never talks about sex, and refuses to read anything that references it. That really narrows her reading choices these days.

I decide to give him the benefit of the doubt. Can I deny him, if ultimately it helps keep his marriage together? Is a little bit of dirty talk on a dating site any worse than him sitting watching porn or reading it?

I'll arrange to meet Ashley when I get home and see if I can figure out where the ground lies, I can always tell her then if needs be.

A new message pops up in my inbox. I shiver in disgust when I read it. It's from a young 17 year old looking after his Aunt's house whilst she's on holiday. He wants to just hook up for sex. He's fiddled the age on the profile so he can view older women.

I block that one. I'm too young to be a Cougar!

The more time I spend on the dating site the more revulsion I feel. I'm sure there are genuine guys on there; they just get lost in amongst the not so genuine sadly.

I decide to reply to a few of the more innocent sounding messages. Perhaps if I can build an online relationship with them I'll get some material for the article I need to write.

Most of them don't want to chat; they want to jump straight into meeting up. I get round that by telling them I'm away with work and won't be back home for several weeks.

I log out with a sense of relief. I don't quite know why but I don't feel comfortable on the site. I'm happy being on my own for the most part. Yes, it would be nice to have some company occasionally for a night out, or just someone to pay you a bit of attention.

I turn and look at the guys on the bus behind me, smiling in the knowledge that for the next seven weeks that isn't going to be an issue.

CHAPTER TWENTY THREE

Alex

The journey to Newcastle is long and boring. I hate being stuck on this minibus. I need to be out in the fresh air.

I keep looking over at Sally. For the first part of the journey her face showed a range of emotions. It must have been something she was reading on her iPad. I'd swear it went from disgust to smiling but there was one point I was convinced she looked scared. I must have got it wrong. Whatever it was that caused it I saw her log out and open her Kindle.

I could watch Sally read for hours. When she's got that thing in her hands you can see the tension leave her shoulders. She relaxes. That thought reminds me of the massage I gave her the other day though. That's not good. I don't need to spend the next few hours sporting a hard on. I try and think of something else. It's impossible. My thoughts never stray far from Sally, and when I think of Sally, I think of the things I'd like to do to her.

I want to slowly undress her. Take my time kissing every part of her body. I'd start at her earlobe; gently biting her collarbone, trail kisses down towards her breasts. Fuck. I need to stop this train of thought before I come in my boxers.

I look out of the window, uninspired by the passing view. It will be a while before we see anything but motorways. All I can see are lines of traffic heading in opposite directions. I try and remember the game I used to play in the car as a child. I'd pick a car and make up a story about the people in it. Who they are. Where they are going. Why they're going there. It helps a little until I glance back over at Sally.

She's biting her lip. I'm screwed. There's a light flush to her face so I can imagine the sort of book she's reading right now.

I need to do something to distract me. Tiny's timing is perfect. He calls from the back of the bus for me to go join the rest of them in a game of cards. I get up and move to join them. I can see the surprise on their faces. In all the time I've toured with them this is the first time I've accepted their invitation to play cards.

I don't have a choice though. I either play cards or I sit there watching Sally, and suffering the hard on from hell.

After just a few minutes I wish I hadn't. They're talking about Sally. Guido seems to think he has a shot with her. I feel sick at the thought of this lothario going anywhere near her. I recognize the emotion as jealousy. How can I be jealous when she doesn't belong to me? Before I can say anything Tiny interrupts him.

"Don't even fucking think about it Guido. Sally's got class and you're not going anywhere near her, do you understand me?" Tiny's voice is firm.

"Sorry, I didn't know you'd claimed first dibs." Guido sniggers. From the look on Tiny's face I don't think that was a good idea. Tiny stands. His large frame fills the space on the minibus. He's easily the biggest one amongst us.

"No one has claimed dibs. No one will be claiming it. You stick to putting your dick in those harlots you love to play around with from the audience. And that goes for the rest of you." He looks around the table at all of us. He's furious. I can see the vein pulsing in his neck. Guido is about to say something else, but he takes in Tiny's stance and wisely thinks twice about it, shutting his mouth quickly.

There's a bunch of mumbled "okay" from around the table.

That settles it then. Tiny's my friend. If he says no one is to go after Sally, then that includes me. I know he's just trying to protect her. He thinks a lot of her. But right now, I really wish he hadn't said that.

CHAPTER TWENTY FOUR

Sally

The guys all seem rather quiet around me when we get off the bus at the hotel in Newcastle. They're normally a lot more jovial, cracking crude jokes and taking the piss. Not today. They must have had a heavy night drinking.

We check in as normal, agreeing to meet in the bar in half an hour. I open the hotel room door and sigh. It's only been a week but already I'm tiring of the plain décor, the minimal furniture. I miss my comfortable sofa. Right now I just want to crash out on my sofa, piled high with cushions, and lose myself in music TV, and my Kindle. But no. We're going out for dinner.

I think I've been out more in this past week than I have in the last year put together. It's a good job Alex and Tiny insist on dragging me along to the gym because all this eating out would play havoc with my waistline otherwise.

I'm hoping I can persuade Alex and Tiny to go to the little tapas bar. I'd gone there when my Mum's friends had invited us before we went to a comedy show at the Arena.

The food was great, the ambience was casual and low key, and the best part is it's only about five minutes walk from where we're staying.

I regret asking them as soon as we walk in. The place is packed. The waitress shows us to a table against the wall. Tiny takes one look at the space between the wall and the table and tells me that Alex and I will have to sit there. He won't fit. He takes the chair opposite us, leaving Alex and I to squeeze onto the sofa style banquette.

The lighting seems a lot lower than the last time I was here as well; it's giving off far too much of a sensual, romantic vibe.

I tell myself I'll be fine. And I am, until the food arrives. The thing with Tapas is that it's a little bit of everything. Lots of bite sized pieces of food. We're provided with knives and forks but for the most part we just use our fingers.

Alex is the most sensual eater I have ever seen. His long fingers dip the food into the sauce, and he licks his fingers clean after he's put it in his mouth.

I've definitely read too many erotic books as all I can imagine when he does this is those fingers pleasuring me, and when he licks his fingers again I almost come on the spot.

I call the waitress over and ask for a glass of iced water. The temperature in here has shot up. I remove my jacket and undo a button on my blouse in an attempt to cool down.

Alex and Tiny exchange a look of confusion. They're both still sitting there with their jackets on.

"Think that last piece of chicken was just a bit too hot for me." I manage to mumble.

Tiny laughs, I love the warm timbre of his laugh, and the way it lights' up his face.

"You're such a wuss. You were fine the other night when we went out for curry." He reminds me.

"Must have just been that piece of chicken." I repeat. "Must have had too much spice on it."

He gives me that fatherly smile he's so fond of using on me. He makes me feel like a little girl at times, bless him. I can just picture him as a father. He's like a big cuddly bear. I feel safe with Tiny.

I wish I could say the same when I'm around Alex. Safe isn't a word I dare use. When I'm around Alex I don't want to be safe. I don't want to be a good girl. I want to act out every fantasy I have from the books that I've read. And that's bad. It's very, very bad.

CHAPTER TWENTY FIVE

Sally

The last few weeks have gone by in a blur. It's been one long cycle of travel – hotel – show – gym - travel. Through it all my attraction to Alex has only heightened if anything.

I've even managed to bring together the bones of the article about the dating site. A couple of the guys that I messaged were happy to share their stories when I mentioned that I was a journalist, as long as names were changed.

There's one guy who's just too busy building his career and travelling with work to find the time to go out and date. He's bright, intelligent, and solvent. He wanted to get to know someone online first, get a feel for her, before he meets up for a chat. He's not looking for long-term commitment. Just a little company. Someone he can take to dinner, and hopefully encourage him to have the odd down day at the beach or just out walking.

If it hadn't been for my unhealthy obsession with Alex I might have been tempted.

Yes, my obsession with Alex is worse than ever. It doesn't matter that I can't have him. The more I know I can't have him, the more I want him. It's like forbidden fruit.

I'm pulled from the article by the sound of the phone ringing. Damn. I hate being interrupted when I'm mid flow writing. I look at the screen to see it's Ashley. I haven't spoken to her since before we set off on tour, so I accept the call.

"Hey sweetie. How are you? Long time no speak." I greet her. In return I can hear sobbing down the phone line. "Ashley. Are you ok? What's wrong? Is the baby okay?" I'm panicking now. This isn't like Ashley. She's normally so cheery.

"It's Gary. He's left me." She sobs even harder.

"What happened?" Even as I ask the question a feeling of dread spreads over me. This has got to be something to do with the dating site and me. I just know it.

"Sally, he kept muttering that it was all your fault. He thinks you said something to me about the dating site he was on. I found it on my own but he won't believe me. I think he's so angry he's going to hurt you Sally."

Shit. That doesn't sound good.

"Never mind me, are you okay?" There are so many questions running through my head right now. Not least is how Ashley found out about the dating site?

"I'll be fine. Honest. You know me. I loved him, but these past few months I've realized he's not the guy I thought he was." She pauses and I can hear her blowing her nose at the other end of the line.

"He started getting aggressive, the way he'd talk to me, and the things he'd ask me to do. I mean come on, I know I'm a bit of a prude but this was just too much." She pauses; I can hear her take in a deep breath before she continues.

"He hit me." Shit. This isn't good. Before I can say anything she continues.

"I knew something wasn't right so I started checking up on him. Nights he said he was working late I'd ring the office and they'd tell me he'd left earlier. I started checking the bank statements and I could see he was eating out and going to hotels but it wasn't with me. He left his laptop open the other day so I checked it and that's when I found the dating site." She breaks down into sobs again.

"He said he was single without kids." She screams down the phone. That had shocked me when I read it, so I can only imagine how much it hurt Ashley.

"Look, I'll be fine. It's you I'm worried about. I've kicked him out, but the way he kept going on about you got me worried. What did he mean?"

Where the hell do I start? It's going to sound like I was condoning what he did now.

"I'm writing an article about a dating site and I came across his profile." Ashley starts to interrupt, but I stop her. "Look, stop, before you say anything. I called him out on it, just in case it was some silly mistake. He said he was only using it for chat. I'm not sure I believed him, but it's not the sort of thing you can tell your friend over the phone is it? I think your husband might be cheating on you. I was going to come tell you as soon as I got back from this stupid tour." I rush the words out before she can interrupt again.

"You should have rung me." I can hear the disappointment in her voice even over the phone line. I'm a terrible friend. Maybe she's right.

"If it had been the other way round would you have told me news like that over the phone? Really?" I ask. Ashley goes quiet for a moment or two.

"No..." she reluctantly offers. "I'd have waited till we were in the same room, and I could have hugged you after I told you." I breathe a huge sigh of relief. I still feel like I'm in the wrong for not telling her, but she's right. That's what I'd planned on doing as soon as I could get to see her.

"Sally. Watch your back, please." She begs. "He won't listen when I tell him it was nothing to do with you. I've never seen him so angry." I can hear the concern for me in her voice.

"I'll be fine. I'm on tour for another couple of weeks still. He'll hopefully have calmed down by the time I get back." I hope that's the case. Gary isn't a small guy; he's taller than me and heavier than me. I've never seen him angry before. But I can imagine. I'll worry about it when I get back, and not before.

We spend over an hour on the phone after that, just chatting about how Ashley's going to manage on her own. She's damned resilient that girl. I offer my baby-sitting services reluctantly. I adore her baby daughter, but I don't have a maternal bone in my body. She's a friend in need though; it's the least I can do.

By the time our conversation ends Ashley seems a lot calmer. I think most of the tears were her worry for my safety. Now I've assured her I'm out of the way and safe it's helped.

I don't have to feel guilty over joining the dating site. It wasn't me that ruined her marriage. It was her husband at the end of the day. As she says, better she finds this out now before her daughter's old enough to understand what's going on.

I suddenly feel homesick for my little house, my friends, and my old life. Being on the road makes everything feel unreal.

The anonymous hotel rooms rob me of my sense of where I am. I could be anywhere. I find myself having to check my diary to see where we are some mornings. As we often stay in the same chain of hotel even the rooms are identical. I'm beginning to feel like a mouse in a wheel, just treading my way around the same path, day after day.

I just need to get through the next two weeks and I can go back to normal.

CHAPTER TWENTY SIX

Sally

I put the phone down and check the calendar. Have I missed the fact today is Friday 13th by any chance? Nope, it's not. Yet after that second phone call I'd be forgiven for thinking it is.

Fred called. He didn't want me to have to wait for the news until I got back to the office. He's very sorry, but once this tour is over, my role at the paper has been made redundant.

He'd come out with the usual platitudes, he'd enjoyed working with me, he's sorry, he's sure I'll land on my feet.

I don't know whether to laugh or cry right now. Can anything else go wrong? I really hope not. I check the time on the phone and realize it's time to head down to reception. I've agreed to meet Alex and Tiny for lunch.

As I'm making sure my hotel room door is locked I hear the click as another door further down the hallway opens. It's Alex's door. I'm about to say hello when I see a scantily clad female leaving his room. I can't hear the conversation between them, but she's touching Alex's arm possessively. He reaches over and gives her a kiss on the cheek before she turns and struts her way back to the elevators.

What. The. Fuck. It can't be. Alex isn't like the rest of the guys. For fuck's sake he's gay. So why did I just see him kissing some skank goodbye.

When I said today couldn't get any worse. I was wrong.

CHAPTER TWENTY SEVEN

Sally

I can't go downstairs. I can't face anyone right now. I slot the card in the door and wait for the green light that shows I can open the door. It doesn't work. I try again but I can't get the card to work. I'm starting to shake from the tears I'm holding in.

I'm trying the card again when I feel a hand reach from behind and take the card from me.

"You've got it the wrong way round." He takes the card, inserts it the other way and the light goes green.

I can't face him right now. The tears are too close to the surface, burning the back of my eyes.

"Aren't you supposed to be coming downstairs for lunch?" he questions.

"Not feeling well." I mumble, rushing into my room. Shit. He's followed me in.

"Anything I can do?" He offers.

"Just leave me alone please. I've had a shitty day, some bad news and I just need to be alone." I crawl onto the bed, hugging the pillow to my chest, trying to hide behind it.

He won't let it go though. I feel the bed sag as he takes a seat at the side of me. He draws me into his arms, and it's almost my undoing.

"Let it out babe, I'm here for you." He offers. If only he was. If only he knew.

I can't stop myself though. I let the tears free. Alex holds me close, which only makes me cry harder.

I cry for my friend. I cry for my job. But, most of all, I cry for Alex.

CHAPTER TWENTY EIGHT

Sally

This is the second time I've found myself tucked into Alex's arms crying my heart out. This isn't me. I'm normally so strong. I don't let things get to me.

I try to tell myself it's just the shock of everything happening all at once, on top of each other.

My sobs slow down but I don't try and move away. Just for a moment I want to stay here, safe in his embrace. To pretend that this is something more. It's childish. It's selfish. Right now I don't care. I need it.

"What happened?" his voice is quiet, gentle.

"Too much. Everything."

"Come on, share it. It will make you feel better, honest." He offers.

So I do. I tell him about the phone call with Ashley, about losing my job. But, I don't tell him how my heart is breaking over him.

Alex looks really concerned when he hears about Gary. I try to tell him it's nothing but he doesn't believe me.

"Promise me you won't go anywhere on your own?" he asks, anxiety in his voice.

"Don't be silly Alex. Gary's not a threat. He's bloody miles away for a start."

Alex puts his hand on my face, forcing me to look at him.

"I'm not messing around Sally. Promise me you won't go anywhere without one of us with you."

"Okay. Okay, if it makes you happy." I mutter. He needn't think I'll be going anywhere with him, that's for sure. It's taking every bit of strength I have just to sit on this bed with him right now.

"We'll work something out about your job. There's got to be loads of papers or magazines that would love to have you on their staff." He sounds so positive when he says it. I'm not so sure. Everywhere is cutting back in this economy. There are reporters out there with a lot more experience than I have that are still out of work.

"Look, come down to lunch. The guys will cheer you up. And we'll work out something. You're one of us now, we always take care of our own." He passes me a tissue. I blow my nose. There's nothing feminine or lady like about it. It sounds more like a bloody elephant.

I look up at the mirror, seeing the mess left behind by my ugly crying session. Ugh. That's going to take some fixing.

Alex doesn't want to leave me alone to even fix my face. He's adamant I'm not even allowed to walk down one flight of stairs on my own. This is bloody ridiculous and I tell him so.

He just gives me that stubborn look of his and ushers me in the direction of the bathroom to sort myself out.

I give in this time, but only because I look as bad as I do. He needn't think I'm listening to him once we're out of this room. He's lost any chance of that after having that girl in his room, that's for sure.

CHAPTER TWENTY NINE

Sally

Lunch is a pretty heated affair. Alex tells the guys I've lost my job when I get home. Eric offers to pull the advertising but as I point out, that would just mean I'd end up going home earlier.

I almost choke on my coffee when Alex tells me he has a spare room I can have if I end up unable to pay my rent. He's telling me that he's on the road a lot so it would be pretty much just me on my own most of the time.

That doesn't help. Being in Alex's house, constant reminders of him, sitting there when he brings one of his boyfriends home. I don't think so. I offer a polite rejection.

"You can rent Alison's flat from her when she moves in with me." Tiny offers. That option I actually give more credence to. "I won't charge you rent till you can afford to pay it." He's such a big brother figure. I don't want to lose touch with him when this tour is over.

"I'm sure I'll be fine." I reply. Actually, I'm not sure I will be, but I'll be damned if I'll let Alex know that.

Then the big goof opens his mouth again. If I were sat any closer I'd kick him under the table.

"There's something else." All eyes turn to him, his voice more serious now than before.

"Sally might be in danger from her friend's ex. He thinks she caused the marriage to break up. We need to make sure one of us is with her at all times. Keep her safe." There's a quick chorus of agreement, followed by a lot of questions.

I end up having to tell them about the whole dating site article. Alex gets a funny expression on his face when I mention the site name, I'm sure he did that when I was talking to Tiny about it before, but I let it pass.

The guys decide for me that I'm not going to be left alone, even to the extent that they'll escort me to and from my room for meals and so on.

"For god's sake guys, give it a bloody rest." I lose my temper. "I don't need babying. I'm a grown woman who's perfectly capable of taking care of herself. I managed it before I met you lot and I'll manage it when this tour is over. Just back off." I stand quickly, knocking my chair back to the floor as I do.

A couple of the other diners look over in concern. I ignore them. Instead I stalk out of the dining room and head back to the elevator.

I can hear Alex try to follow me, and then Tiny's murmur telling him to leave me be. Thank fuck for that.

When I get into my room I lose it. My temper that is. I pick up anything that's not breakable and throw it. Surprisingly that really does make me feel better.

The room looks like a hurricane blew through it when I hear a tapping at the door.

"Fuck off!" I shout. I don't want to see any of them right now. They can take their he-man behavior and piss off as far as I am concerned.

"Sally, come on, let me in." I hear Tiny's voice on the other side of the door. He sounds disappointed. Reluctantly I open the door to him, I leave it ajar and return to the room, my back to him.

I cringe when I see the state of the room.

"What's going on Sally? This isn't like you?" Tiny asks. "I get that you're upset over your job, but you seem to be taking it harder than I would have thought. Are you scared of this Gary bloke?"

He hasn't a clue thank god. He still thinks this temper tantrum is about a job or a stupid bully, not a broken heart. How the hell can I have a broken heart when I wasn't even in a relationship with Alex?

"I just can't stand this macho bullshit Tiny. You know me well enough by now to know I can't stand being treated like a bloody child."

I sit down on the end of the bed, the energy rush from trashing the room now gone.

"It was just one thing too much today, that's all. Everything got on top of me. I'm sorry."

The bed dips as Tiny sits down next to me, almost tipping me to the floor, as I have to shift over to accommodate him. He puts his arm around me and draws me into a hug. Tiny gives brilliant hugs. In his arms I feel safe and protected.

"Come on girl, let's get you out of here. I'll help you clear this mess up later." He offers. That sounds like a good idea right now.

We head off outside to explore yet another town that I've forgotten the name of, that looks like every other town we've been to with it's chain of coffee stores and mobile phone shops. Right now this anonymity is just what I need. It means I don't have to think. I can just cruise along.

And that's what I do for the rest of the afternoon. I cruise along, refusing to think about what the future contains, or rather what it doesn't. I decide I'll worry about that another day.

CHAPTER THIRTY

Sally

I feel a little better after my walk with Tiny. I've calmed down some. I feel a little bit more like myself now.

I declined joining the guys for dinner. I just can't face it before the show tonight. Instead I order a meal from the bar and take it back to my room.

There's a notification on my phone when I check it from the guy I've been chatting with on the dating site – *JamesT89*. That bloody site is responsible for half my problems right now. I almost don't log on, but sod it. I enjoy chatting with him.

Hey. How was your day?

How do I answer that? Honest?

My day sucked. Let's not talk about it. Tell me again why I still can't see your photo?

I know I'm pushing my luck, but I just need to know I'm not talking to some fat, balding businessman. That would be the last straw today.

I told you, I don't want people from work to recognize me. It could cause problems. Tell me what I can do to cheer you up?

Argh. I hate that he can see what I look like, but I don't know about him. Still it does mean I didn't make a snap judgment based on an image. I'm guilty of doing that with some of the people the site has suggested for matches.

Just talk to me about your day, take my mind off mine. It's nothing I want to share right now.

I need to escape for a little while. I check the clock to make sure I'm still okay for time.

Nothing interesting. Had a sports massage this morning. Had lunch with the guys I work with.

We talk about nothing and everything for the next half hour before we both have to sign off for work. I love that he even seems to have the same odd work pattern as me some days. The talking about nothing, things that were totally outside of what I'm going through right now was good for me.

I bristle as I hear the knock at the door. One of the guys has arrived to 'escort' me to the venue. It's Tiny. Now there's a surprise. I do love him but this unofficial bodyguard crap is wearing thin already.

I grab my jacket and notebook and follow him reluctantly to the elevator. I feel like a naughty child being escorted everywhere.

***

This is the part of the show I dislike the most. The one where they choose four audience members to come up on stage and get lap dances from four of the dancers.

Eric goes out on stage to ask for volunteers. There's a girl on crutches that he was a bit reluctant to accept, but she was so eager he gave in. She's hobbling her way to the stage as he looks around the audience. I don't see it but from the reaction one girl has flashed her breasts at him. She gets picked.

I hear Eric's voice over the sound system as he politely thanks another girl who obviously decided to flash her arse to get picked. He advises her that she was a little over eager.

He picks a girl from the other side of the audience then turns to me and winks before announcing that he gets to pick the final candidate.

I'm curious. I can see him scanning the audience and wonder what skanky candidate will be next. I'm startled when the spotlight that's following his hand stops on a man who seems over eager to come up to the stage.

One of the guys is not going to be pleased that's for sure!

Eric goes down the row of chairs, asking each audience member to introduce themselves and who they'd like to dance for them.

The girl on crutches is called Helen and she'd love to have Guido dirty dance on her. The next girl, the boob flasher is Kelly. When asked who she want's she bluntly replies "I don't care who as long as he puts his cock in my mouth." Behind me I hear the guys groaning. This isn't what they want to hear. It normally leads to stalking after the show.

Eric turns to the next woman, she's high pitched and screechy when she tells us she's another Kelly and she'll take some of what she's having please.

This leaves the guy at the end of the row. I'd expect that a guy pulled from the audience would be reluctant to be on stage, but no, this guy's the total opposite.

"I'll take the cock in my mouth and add a cock up my arse as well mate." My mouth drops open in shock.

"Shit. I'm not doing him." I hear Guido muttering. "Alex should be in this fucking routine not me." He continues. That's a bit harsh. He can tell I'm not impressed from the glare that I give him.

"I'm getting too old for this shit." Rick complains. The rest murmur their agreement. I have to laugh. I don't think one of them is over 25.

The music to Dirty by Christina Aguilera comes on. The guys walk out onto the stage as the talk intro comes on and move in front of their allocated audience member.

They make a show of pulling shiny silver handcuffs from the back of their police trousers and fasten their fan's hands behind the back of the chairs.

At least this way they know they won't get groped.

They dance around the chairs erotically, occasionally coming close and dry humping closer to the chairs.

Every time the song has the word dirty they pretend to wipe the sweat from their faces.

At the rap section they stand with their backs to the chairs, unfastening and fastening their black police shirts. They've gone with the US style uniform as it fits much more closely to the skin than the English counterpart. By the time the chorus is back the shirts are discarded and the guys are strutting up and down around the stage.

The guys do a series of kicks; hump the stage, and hip swivels before walking backwards and rubbing their arses in the seated faces. This does nothing for me but the girls and the guy out on that stage love it.

This isn't a full strip routine; they just strip down to boxer briefs. It's a popular end to the first half of the show.

I've never seen the guys look so relieved as they do when they come off stage.

"I feel dirty." Rick complains, rushing for the dressing room. I'm not surprised. The girl he was dancing for took every opportunity she could to reach over and put her mouth on him whenever he came close enough.

I hear the blast of the shower from the dressing room. I don't go in. I learned my lesson the other week when I walked in just as Alex was dropping his trousers. Holy hotness.

There's a bellow from the dressing room and we all rush in. There's a very naked Rick standing there, covering his modesty with his hands. He's dripping wet. In front of him is the girl from the audience he was dancing for.

Eric shouts outside the door for security as Tiny grabs her arm to take her outside.

"Can't I even have a fucking shower in peace without these crazy fans following me in there." Rick pleads. "I'm sick of them offering to service me." He moans.

This should be funny, a male stripper standing there naked and dripping wet, complaining about over eager fans but for some reason it isn't.

I don't know about the rest of them but previously I'd always felt safe in the backstage area of the theaters. Out front is different. We expect this to happen out there. But back here is our space, where we're supposed to be free from the chaos.

Security arrives and leads the girl away. Eric complaining to them all the while that this shouldn't have been allowed to happen.

Rick shrugs it off and heads back to his shower. They don't have a lot of spare time in the interval after all. The guys start changing, seemingly oblivious to my presence in the room. I hurry out before I see anything else I don't need to see.

CHAPTER THIRTY ONE

Sally

The incident in the interval at the theater combined with the guys over protective macho bullshit gave me a terrible nightmare. It's one of those nonsensical one's where the lines between reality and fantasy become blurred.

I can't remember it clearly when I wake but the bits I can remember are confusing. Alex was there, dressed as white knight astride his charger. Gary was there but as some sort of grotesque monster. Tiny resembled Dumbledore, the wrinkled old wizard from Harry Potter. There was some sort of fight over me as I recall before Dumbledore grabbed me and we flew off on a large golden eagle. Now that reminded me of Gandalf in Lord of The Rings. What a twisted dream. I've no idea what my subconscious was trying to tell me with that one.

I open my phone to check the time and see I have another message from James on the dating site. That's not like him; he often goes days between messages. It's one reason I feel so comfortable talking to him, as he's not pushy at all.

Morning beautiful, hope you slept well after your bad day yesterday.

Is he some sort of psychic? I reply and let him know I had a crazy nightmare, but don't share the details. Instead we spend a few moments talking about a new song in the charts that we both like.

I excuse myself and let him know I'll chat later. Right now I need to go grab a shower before breakfast. We've got a slightly longer journey today so I need to get packed as well. We don't have much time.

Breakfast is a lot lighter hearted than yesterday's lunch. The guys are in a silly mood, taking the mickey out of Rick for the shower incident. Guido makes a comment about his sexual prowess with the fans that have us all in stitches.

"You're so conceited." I tell him.

He looks affronted. "I'm not conceited. I can have any woman I want, any time I want. I'm a Naked Night's stripper." He says this with such a straight face we all burst into laughter. The older couple seated at the next table look affronted at his words. That only makes us all laugh louder.

I might not have had a great night's sleep, but I do feel better today. There's nothing that can't be fixed. I'll find a new job, and if needs be I'll find a new home. My friend is fine.

The only thing that's not fine is my unhealthy obsession for Alex, but in less than two weeks we'll have parted ways and I'll be able to get over it. I can survive two weeks. Can't I?

CHAPTER THIRTY TWO

Sally

The past week has dragged. It's been a routine of gym, travel, hotel, show, gym, travel, hotel, and show. I'm not performing and I'm shattered. I've no idea how the guys find the stamina for this.

Places have blended into each other to the point I've no idea where we are most days, but today we're arriving in Edinburgh. This is one city I'm looking forward to. I've been warned I won't get much time for sight seeing. We have a free evening tonight as it was such a long journey to get here, but the boys will be busy rehearsing most of tomorrow and they still won't let me out without one of my 'keepers' as they call them.

Dan pulls the bus up on Princes Street, not far past the station. Our Travelodge is just behind this huge shopping street. We start unloading the bags before Dan goes off to wherever he's arranged to park.

I've managed a few conversations with him when the boys were distracted. He's told me that compared to some of the 'talent' he drives around my guys are pretty tame.

He's driven actors, rock groups and corporate and some of the requests are hilarious. He's too professional to tell me most of them or name them, but shares the requests for particular brands of alcohol, water or food. I dread to think what he's seen in that rear view mirror of his some days. He winks as he tells me that he also has a camera monitoring the back of the minibus. I wonder how many wannabe rock stars and groupies have been caught out on that? He won't tell me, no matter what I bribe him with.

"You know, that Alex is a good guy." He tells me with a wink as he's handing me my luggage. Alex is standing on the pavement waiting to walk me to the hotel. "You two would make a cute couple."

"Yeah, shame he's gay." I mumble. I don't know what I said, but Dan bursts out into loud, jovial laughter and walks off back towards the front of the bus.

Alex walks over and takes my bag from me. I hate it when he does that. I'm not a feminist by any means; I think it's just one more piece of control they've taken away from me lately. I feel smothered.

Just a few doors down from the hotel there's a little pub nestled in the corner of Rose Street. It's like an alley full of little treats hidden behind the huge main shopping avenue. There's just enough sunlight creeping down between the tall buildings to make it pleasant enough to sit outside.

We're all here although Tiny is looking a touch uncomfortable trying to fit his large frame into the too small chairs.

It's a glorious day; Edinburgh really does shine in the sun. I've not been here for a few years now. I make a mental note to come back and do the tourist thing another day.

The guys are excited that there's only another week of the show left. They're talking about what they're going to do when they're finished.

Rick and Jonny have booked a trip to Amsterdam to see the girls and Guido and Jackal are considering joining them.

Eric is going down to Norfolk to spend some time with his Mum. She sounds like a lovely lady.

Tiny glows as he talks about the plans he and Alison have to decorate their new house. They bought it together just before the tour started and she's moving in when it's ready. He repeats the offer of me renting Alison's flat if I need it.

Alex stays quiet during all this. He keeps casting sideways glances at me. I guess that it's because I'm not joining in. When this tour ends in a week I'll have nothing left. No job, and pretty soon no house as I only have enough saved to cover a couple of months rent. I still don't know what I want to do, or who to approach for work.

I've been checking the job ads but there's nothing there that I'm qualified for. To be honest for most of them I'm over qualified and know they'd never consider me.

The only light has been my chats with James on the dating site. We have so much in common. Strangely he's never suggested we meet up when I get home, and I'm not sure if I'm ready for that anyway.

The main problem is that he's not Alex. No matter how much time passes I can't seem to get over this lust. I know it can't be love, it's far too soon, but what I wouldn't give to scratch that itch just the once.

As usual just thinking about Alex taking me to bed makes me flushed and uncomfortable. Tiny notices.

"Are you okay Sally?"

"Yeah, just a little stir crazy I guess. I think I need some fresh air, and I wouldn't mind hitting a few of those shops on Princes Street." I look at the guys, hoping for once that they'll let me go on my own. Guys hate shopping right?

No such luck. Alex jumps to his feet and offers me his arm. I want to scream in frustration, but I want to go check out the shops so I accept it.

I draw in a breath when we emerge out onto the main street. The sheer volume of people walking past is breathtaking. I'm not used to this much human traffic, it's a little daunting really.

I look up and in front of me see the massive structure of the Castle. It looks amazing. I know we haven't got time to go there this trip, but I really would like to come back and see it one day.

The stores on the main street are the same ones I'd find in any town in the country, the difference here being their size. They're huge! I feel dwarfed by the buildings and the sheer volume of people.

As much as I dislike having to have a minder, I'm slightly grateful to have Alex with me so I don't get pulled into the crowd.

I spot La Senza and head for it. I expect Alex to wait outside; it's a sexy lingerie store after all. No such luck. He follows me in.

"Alex." I turn on him.

"What?" He hasn't got a clue.

"You can't be here."

"Why not?" He really has no clue.

"Alex, I need to buy underwear. To do that I need a little privacy." My voice rises slightly at the end. I'm embarrassed that he's here and we're even having this conversation.

"I'm fine in here." He turns to the rack on his left and lifts up a bra. "This would look great on you."

I'm about to express my indignation when I look at what he's holding. Wow, it's exactly what I'd wear, and when I take it from him I'm surprised to see it's the right size. Fluke.

He reaches for the matching knickers, and once again they're the right size. Another fluke. Typical, when I shop for lingerie on my own they never seem to have my size unless I ask an assistant to go get it from out back for me.

Alex wanders over to another rack and passes me another set. Again they're the right size and they're perfect for me.

"Erm, thank you. I. I. I need to go try these on. Can you wait here?" I rush for the changing room at the back of the store.

They fit perfectly. Wearing these I feel hot. I look at the price ticket and frown. I can't afford both of them. In truth I can barely afford one of them, having lost my job. I contemplate returning them both to the shelf and trying my luck in Primark instead. I could probably get a new set of lingerie for every day of the week in there for what just one of these sets would cost me.

Common sense wins over. I can't afford luxuries like these anymore. I'm handing them back to the assistant when I feel them taken from my hand. It's Alex.

"Alex! I need to put them back. They're not right for me." He just gives me a look, ignores me and walks over to the till with them. Before I can get to him he's handed over his card and the transaction is over. Damn.

I follow him out of the store, dragging my feet. I'm not enjoying my shopping trip anymore.

Alex hands me the bag. "Look, it's a gift. I know they'll have looked great on you. And I also know you saw the price tags and sacrificed something nice for the bloody rent. So here, they're my treat."

How the hell does he know so much about me? It must be a gay thing. I hesitantly take the bag from him.

"By the way." He throws over his shoulder as he walks a little ahead of me. "Bet you look hot as hell in that black one."

I stand there a moment, wishing the ground would open up and swallow me. Receiving a compliment like that from a straight guy would be sexy as hell, but a gay guy? It just doesn't feel quite right.

CHAPTER THIRTY THREE

Alex

I'd love to see Sally model the lingerie I just bought for her. She was mortified when I went in the shop with her. I couldn't resist. I've got a picture in my minds eye of what she'll look like in it.

She never commented on me picking the right size. I don't think she realizes how much I know about her. For some reason she seems to treat me like a big brother. I wish she wouldn't, but if that's all I can get from her then I'll take it, gratefully.

I know her size from the times I've been in her room, massaging the aches away for her, or just holding her close when she'd break down and cry. I'm not a stalker. Leastways I hope I'm not stalking her. I just like to be around her.

She's walking by my side when I hear her gasp. I turn and she's gone deathly pale.

"What's wrong?" I look around us, seeking out whatever seems to have shocked her so badly, but I don't see anything out of place.

She draws her shoulders back and puts on a brave face as she assures me nothing is wrong. I don't know why, but I don't believe her. I have a sense that tells me something is very wrong. I just can't pinpoint what.

"You know what?" She says. "I think I'm more tired than I realized. Can we just head back to the hotel?"

That settles it. Something has definitely spooked her. I take another look around, still seeing nothing obvious.

The relief in her face when I agree to go back to the hotel is obvious. I'm going to get to the bottom of this.

Sally

It can't be. It must just be a figment of my imagination. I shake my head to clear the image from it. I could have sworn I just saw Gary in the street ahead of me.

Alex has noticed something is wrong, but I can't tell him. They'd never let me out at all if I told him.

It can't be Gary. We're hours away from home, and there's no reason for him to be here in Edinburgh. It must just be that lookalike thing, the one where they say all of us have a double.

Alex agrees that we can head back to the hotel and I sigh in relief. It's just my overactive imagination but I'll sure feel better when I'm back in my room.

CHAPTER THIRTY FOUR

Sally

The guys have decided that we're all going out tonight to a bar called Ghillie Dhu. It's at the far end of Princes Street and we're walking, so I select my flat, comfortable shoes. It's a Friday night so I go for smart jeans and a sheer black blouse that shows off the lace camisole I'm wearing underneath. It's quite low cut, and with the bra that Alex bought me, really shows off my bust.

I'm thinking it's a little too much when there's a knock at the door signaling the arrival of the latest bodyguard. I sigh in resigned frustration. I've got used to it now, but it doesn't mean I've learned to accept it yet.

Tiny stands there, looking hot in a dark shirt, jeans and a black jacket. He offers me his arm, and I take it. Like the gentleman he is he escorts me down to the bar where everyone else is already gathered and waiting for me.

"About bloody time." Guido mutters, then looks up at me, and his jaw drops.

"Bloody hell, Sally. You scrub up well." Being Guido I take it as the compliment I think it is. There's a murmur of agreement from the rest of them. Maybe the top wasn't inappropriate after all. Then I remember the type of girls these guys are used to and panic again.

"You look lovely." Alex whispers in my ear. I didn't hear him come up beside me and it startles me a little. "You look good enough to eat." I take a deep breath at the mental image I have of Alex 'eating' me. My face must flush a little and Alex just laughs.

In the early evening Edinburgh is still a hustle and bustle of people. I'd expected that it would have quieted down, but if anything it feels busier.

I settle into people watching as we walk along. I have a bad habit of making stories up about the people that pass, imagining where they're rushing off to, where they've come from. An idea starts to form in my mind. If I don't manage to get a new job when I get home, perhaps I could start to write a book. It's something I've wanted to do for a long time. And being with these guys for the past seven weeks has ensured that I wouldn't be short of material.

We cross the road and find ourselves outside Ghillie Dhu. It looks a little like an old Methodist church from the outside. We've got a table booked to eat here, before a Ceilidh style party upstairs later in the evening. The interior is dark, yet not gloomy. There's a certain ambience to it.

We're shown to a booth against the back wall, a long cushioned U shape booth. I find myself squished in between Alex and Tiny as usual. Sometimes these two take this whole bodyguard thing just a step too far.

The food is enjoyable, but the company is better. Away from the anonymity of the Travelodge, and the pressure of rehearsals and performing the guys relax.

They're talking about finding a beauty salon in the morning to top up their fake tans, although if Guido gets sprayed anymore I'm afraid he'll look like a tangerine, he's orange enough as it is.

We're laughing and joking and having a good time. For a few hours I can forget about losing my job, and just enjoy being me, and spend some time with these new friends of mine.

I may not like the way some of them carry on, sleeping with all and sundry, but apart from that I do really like them as people. I feel safe and comfortable around them. There's a lot to be said for that.

Guido and Jackal come back from the bathroom grinning from ear to ear. Apparently the male toilets here are stainless steel buckets rather than urinals. That sounds a little disgusting until Guido shows me the picture he took on his phone. They look amazing. Very modern and sleek compared to the rustic feel of the bar.

We make our way up the curving stone staircase to the upper bar where the dancing will be. There's a long narrow bar against one wall and the guys decide I need to start drinking whisky; we are in Scotland after all.

The whisky burns a little going down, but then fills me with a lovely warm glow. I could get used to this. After a few of these I can tell I'm starting to feel a little tipsy. They're a lot stronger than my normal Tia Maria. Despite the flat shoes I stumble a little and fall into Alex. He straightens me with his arm, and pulls me close into his side, holding me there protectively.

"Easy there, Sally." He croons. "You might want to slow it down a little." He doesn't release his hold, and unsure if it's the whisky or bravado I never thought I had, I nestle in close. Just for a few moments I want to pretend. My body is on fire where it touches his.

I know it's the whisky when I feel like I want to take my finger and trace it along his strong jawline. Thankfully, I'm not that drunk that I follow through. Part of me wishes I were.

The band starts to play and Alex drags me onto the floor behind him. I'm about to protest when the others join us.

I've no idea what I'm doing but it's hard not to get drawn in by the music. Pretty soon we're all clapping along and swinging around on each other's arms. I'm thrown from partner to partner. I can't catch my breath from it all. It's exhilarating.

The music ends suddenly and I'm standing there, captured in Alex's arms.

I lose all sense of my surroundings, finding myself drowning in the depths of his eyes instead. I'm just about to open my mouth and say something stupid, like how much of a shame it is that he's gay when I'm rescued by Tiny, bearing another whisky shot glass.

I down the shot in one. I don't remember any of the evening after that.

CHAPTER THIRTY FIVE

Alex

I'm not sure just how much Sally drank tonight but she can barely walk. Between us Tiny and I get her back to her hotel room. She's still humming one of the Ceilidh tunes. She may be drunk, but she's had a good evening.

I rummage through her purse until I find her hotel room key, and open the door while Tiny physically lifts her up and carries her over to her bed.

She's out of it.

"I'll stay and watch her for a while, make sure she doesn't throw up." I suggest to Tiny. He looks at the limp form on the bed and agrees it wouldn't be a bad idea.

I pull the armchair over from the window and settle into it. I'm content just to sit here and watch her sleep. The low rise and fall of her chest reassures me she's fine. She's going to have a hell of a bad head in the morning though, especially after all that whisky.

I'm so grateful there's less than a week of the tour left. Spending every day with her is killing me. I promised Tiny, along with the other guys, that we'd leave her alone. Right now that's the last thing I want to do.

Sally stirs on the bed, she looks uncomfortable. I move over and slowly remove her shoes. I hesitate before removing her jeans, but they can't be comfortable. I open the button and draw them down slowly so as not to wake her.

Crap. She's wearing the black lace that I bought her today. She looks even better in it than I visualized.

I remove her jeans and fold them neatly on the dressing table. I want to trace my fingers all over her delicate skin. I want to draw aside those lacy knickers and explore her hidden depths.

Shit. I can't do this. As much as I want to touch her, I want her to be fully awake when I do. This is wrong. I throw a blanket over her bottom half to keep her warm, and return to the chair. I sit there intending to watch her all night, but at some time I must fall asleep because her cursing wakes me.

"What the hell are you doing in my room Alex!" she gasps. It's obviously too much for her hung-over head as she goes very pale, very quiet and holds her head in her hands.

"What the hell is wrong with me?" she whispers.

"Whisky hangover." I offer. "I did warn you to slow it down a little." I chuckle. One look at her poor face and I go quiet. She's gone green. I've heard of it happening but never seen it.

Sally makes a dash for the bathroom and I hear the sound of her throwing up. Part of me wants to go in there and help her, to hold the hair away from her face and to wipe her down with a cool cloth to help her feel better. But this is Sally we're talking about. She does have a bit of a temper on her at times and I'm rather too fond of my balls to have her threaten them if I see her like this.

Sod it. She's a damsel in distress. I head for the bathroom anyway.

She's finished throwing up when I get there and is leaning on the sink with her hands. Her head leant over, hair shielding her face from view.

"I'm dying." She mutters.

"You're not dying. You're just experiencing a whisky hangover is all. They can be pretty brutal. Best thing for you is a big fried breakfast and a session down at the gym." Her face pales at the thought of food. The mention of the gym makes her throw me a look of utter disgust.

"If you think I'm going anywhere other than my bed today you're sadly mistaken." She moves to sit on the closed toilet seat. It's then that she notices she's only wearing her sheer blouse and underwear.

"Where are my clothes?" She sounds worried. "Who undressed me?"

"You looked uncomfortable, so I just took your jeans off." She looks up at me, as though she's just realizing something.

"What are you doing in my room?"

"I spent the night." She's just about to throw a fit when I add on the end. "In the chair. Nothing happened."

"No, well it bloody wouldn't would it?" I'm confused by her words, is that disappointment I hear in her tone? More likely it just means that I'm the last man she'd think of sleeping with. I've really got to get over this obsession I have with her.

I leave her to shower and freshen up for breakfast, refusing to take no for an answer. I also tell her she's coming to the gym with Tiny and me as well.

She looks disgusted at the idea but doesn't say no. I think she's resigned herself to just doing what she's told today. I miss the fire of her usual retorts.

I head back to my room for my own shower, although mine will need to be a cold one.

My hard on didn't dissipate all night knowing that beneath that blanket she was wearing nothing more than a strip of black lace. I'm seriously in need of releasing this tension.

CHAPTER THIRTY SIX

Sally

I've got a few minutes before Alex comes back to escort me to breakfast so I log onto the dating site to see if I have any more messages.

There are a couple of new messages from guys I'm not familiar with and they get quickly deleted. Do they not read profiles? They're after one night stands and are a bit too graphic in what they'd like to do with me. I block them while I'm at it.

I smile when I see another message from James.

> *Morning beautiful, hope you slept well.*
> *How's Edinburgh treating you?*

I tell him that Edinburgh has treated me to my first, and last whisky hangover. He sends an 'lol' message in return. Very helpful James. Not. I send a 'pffft' in response. We're normally much more articulate than that.

I'll be back in York in a week or so. Think you will be too.

Do you fancy meeting up for a quiet drink?

Shit. How do I respond to that? Part of me wants to meet James. We connect on so many levels, have a lot of things in common, and share the same sense of humor. But part of me feels safe and confident behind the screen. Would that translate into meeting him for real?

I'm not sure. I love our chats on here, but I still don't even know what you look like? You could be Quasimodo for all I know. Lol. x

I hope he takes that the right way. He hasn't replied by the time Alex knocks on my door to take me to breakfast. I'm not sure whether that makes me relieved or disappointed.

CHAPTER THIRTY SEVEN

Sally

Tiny is a little the worse for wear as well this morning, as are most of the guys with the exception of Alex. Even the normally sober Eric looks a little green around the gills today.

Because he's hung-over Tiny decides to hit the heavy weights in an attempt to sweat it off. That means he delegates my training to Alex.

Alex is wearing a tight white vest, and short black shorts. I may be hung-over, but I'm not dead and my internal voice is having a field day telling me what she'd like to do to that body in bed.

This is going to be a long session. I groan. Luckily Alex mistakes it for a hangover groan.

We're fine starting the routine off as normal with the treadmill and the cardio stretches. I'm even starting to feel slightly less embarrassed about them now. That's partly helped because I'm already starting to look a little more toned than when we started, and for some reason there are a lot of large people in the gym this morning.

Alex passes me the boxing gloves and puts the pads on his hands. This might not be too bad. Perhaps I can use this boxercise set to exorcise some of my sexual frustration.

I think I must have misheard Alex, so ask him to repeat himself.

"I'm not Quasimodo you know." What the hell does he mean? I continue punching side-to-side trying to figure out what he just said.

He realizes I don't understand him and continues.

"I'm JamesT89." My punches slow a little as understanding begins to dawn.

"But you can't be!" I state. I increase the speed of the punches, but now I'm putting a lot more force into them.

My brain is too messed up to understand what he's trying to tell me. It can't be what I think it is.

"We'll be back in York in a week, and I can ask you out properly then."

It can't be, but it is. Alex is JamesT89, the anonymous guy that I've been chatting to on the dating site for the last few weeks. That's why he has that funny expression on his face whenever the dating site is mentioned. That's why he doesn't have a profile photo. I go back through our conversations, trying to see how I didn't spot it. He was clever; he never lied. I just interpreted a lot of what he said in the wrong context.

Then another thought dawns, just as I'm hitting an upper cut thrust to the pads.

"But you can't be. You're gay!" I state confidently.

Alex drops his hands at the word gay, surprised. Unfortunately for Alex my brain hasn't quite caught up and my left hand continues the path of the upper cut movement it was in and connects with his chin. The force knocks him backwards into the wall. He bangs his head and slides down the wall into a heap.

Oh my god! I think I've killed him. I stand there looking down at the crumpled form and start screaming for Tiny at the top of my voice.

CHAPTER THIRTY EIGHT

Sally

Tiny comes rushing over just as Alex is trying to rise to his feet.

"What the hell happened?" Tiny asks me. I flinch under his stare. He looks furious. He helps Alex the rest of the way to his feet. Alex is rubbing the back of his head where it hit the wall.

"I hit him." I whisper.

"I can see that Sally, but why?" I'm still a little too shocked to understand quite what just happened.

"He moved the pads." I offer petulantly.

"She thinks I'm gay." Alex mutters. I'm so relieved I haven't killed him I sob.

Tiny just looks confused. "But you are gay you daft lad. Let's get you looked over." He reaches for Alex's arm to guide him to the front desk but it's rudely brushed away.

"What the fuck?" Alex splutters. "Why does everyone suddenly think I'm fucking gay?" He's a bit cross to say the least.

Tiny ignores Alex and starts to drag him to the front desk, asking for their first aider.

The first aider quickly arrives and takes Alex and Tiny into the coffee area to check out Alex's head. I'm left standing in reception looking like a lost soul.

"Are you alright miss?" the employee on the desk asks me.

"Erm. I think so, just a little shocked and surprised is all." I'm trying to peer through the tiny window set in the door but can't get the angle right.

"Don't worry about it. It happens all the time, simple slip of concentration. He'll be fine." She assures me. "Go on through, grab yourself a coffee with plenty of sugar. It's good for the shock." She gestures towards the coffee lounge where they've taken Alex.

I'm not sure I can go in there right now. I'm struggling to take in what Alex told me just before I almost knocked him out. He can't be James. James is a guy on a dating site. James isn't gay.

Suddenly it all becomes too much for me. I need to get out of here. I grab the contents of my locker and head off back to the hotel; I'll shower there. I can't be here right now.

I'm almost back at the hotel when my mind starts playing tricks on me again. I'm convinced that I see Gary walking towards me, a scowl on his face. I blink to clear the vision. He's disappeared, if he was ever there.

Instead, rushing towards me from the hotel is Guido.

"Sally, thank god you're okay." He sounds so relieved. "What possessed you to come back on your own? You know you need one of us with you at all times."

"Oh fuck off, Guido. I'm so sick of all this macho bullshit you lot keep coming out with. I'm a fucking grown woman who's perfectly capable of taking care of herself." I'm furious. I know even as I'm saying the words that they're too harsh and I see the truth of it as Guido's face falls. I know I should apologize, but I can't. Right now I just need to get back to my room and try and work out what the hell is going on.

CHAPTER THIRTY NINE

Sally

The pounding on my door won't go away. I try and ignore it but it just keeps going on and on. I hear Tiny's voice above it.

"Sally, open the bloody door. I know you're in there. Sally."

Reluctantly, I give up. He's not going to go away and the sooner I get this over and done with the better. I know he's going to be furious with me, first for hitting Alex so hard he almost passed out, and then for leaving the gym on my own.

I open the door slowly; it's too slow for Tiny as he pushes against it to get into the room quicker.

"Nice to see you too." I mutter sarcastically.

"I could kill you, you stupid woman." He glares at me. "Don't ever pull a stunt like that again. Do you know how scared I was?" Oh, he's chosen to lead with that rather than me almost knocking his friend out. That's interesting.

"I'm a grown woman Tiny. I can take care of myself. I'm tired of being treated like a bloody naughty child. I've done nothing wrong, and yet I feel like I'm being continually punished." I glower.

"Sally, we're just trying to keep you safe. We care about you is all." His face falls a little. Damn. I hate it when he looks like that. It makes me feel like a right bitch.

"Okay, I'm sorry, I shouldn't have done it. I just couldn't stay there any longer." I feel the bed behind my knees and collapse down onto it.

"Aren't you going to ask how Alex is?" he looks at me.

"Nope, I assume he's fine or you wouldn't be here berating me." I still sound like a petulant child.

"He's going to be fine. He'll have a bit of a bump on the back of his head for a few days that will be a bit sore but he's lucky you didn't give him a black eye." He laughs at that last bit. "Eric would have killed him for turning up to a show with a black eye."

I giggle, but it's more of a relieved, nervous giggle than anything.

"Good." That's the only word I can think of right now. I'm still trying to get my head around the whole Alex/James scenario.

Part of me is relieved that they're one and the same but the other part of me, that other part is furious at the deception.

"That's all you've got to say? He told me what happened. I think you two need to talk." Tiny stands in front of me, towering over me as I'm sat on the bed.

"There's nothing to talk about. He deceived me and he's gay. I'll get over it." I huff.

"Yeah. Well. Turns out I might have been misinformed." Tiny looks guilty as I look up at him.

"Misinformed about what?"

"Misinformed about the fact that Alex is gay." He mumbles. "Turns out he's absolutely not gay and has it pretty bad for you." Tiny laughs. I look up at him in surprise.

Did he really just say that Alex isn't gay? I must have misheard him.

"So, will you talk to him? Please" Tiny pleads.

"What is this? Some kind of playground fun? Your best mate fancies a girl and sends you to tell her?" I'm a little indignant now. The whole thing just smacks of the school playground boys mentality. "Not today, Tiny. Not today." I mutter. "Not anytime soon. Can you leave me alone now please?"

My head is still fuzzy from last night's alcohol. That must be it. In fact, I almost convince myself I'm dreaming this whole silly episode until I pinch myself. Ouch. That bloody hurt.

"Sally." Tiny is pleading with me. This huge giant of a man is pleading with me. I stay resolved.

"No. I don't want to see anyone right now. I've got some thinking to do."

I stand and gently push Tiny towards the door, grateful that he allows it. I'd not be able to move him otherwise.

"Just give him a chance Sally." He begs. "It's bad enough his friends made such a huge mistake. Don't let him lose you as well." He places a gentle kiss on my forehead as he leaves the room.

CHAPTER FORTY

Sally

I must have dozed off as I'm woken by the ping of the message app on my iPad. Part of me doesn't want to open it. I suspect I know who it will be, and I'm not sure I'm ready for it.

I've lusted after him since almost the first time I met him. But lusting after someone you think you can't have is a whole different ballgame to lusting after someone who apparently wants you too. That makes it scary. That makes it real.

Sure enough it's a message from James.

I'm sorry. I didn't know the guys thought I was gay! I just didn't want to rush you and scare you away. I wanted to wait until we were home and we could do this properly. I never meant to deceive you. Please talk to me. xxx

I don't know how to reply. Right now I'm scared. I'm scared that for once in my life I might actually have a chance at being happy. And yes, that is scary. Because if I'm honest with myself, I don't think I've ever been truly happy before.

I'm scared that if I turn down this opportunity, then I might never get another one. I'm torn.

I pick up the phone and dial the internal extension. He answers on the second ring.

"Can we talk?" I ask.

"I'll be right there." He hangs up.

Moments later there's a knock on my door. I open it to let Tiny in. He looks at me with such compassion in his eyes that a stray tear starts to fall down my cheek.

"I don't know what to do." I cry.

"It's okay sweet girl. We'll make it right, I promise."

He pulls me into a hug, and in his large, muscled arms I feel safe and loved. I know if anyone can help me sort this out, this bear of a man can.

He sits on the bed and draws me onto his lap. We spend the rest of the afternoon talking; all the while he's running his hand up and down my back, soothing me like a scared child.

He reminds me that Alex is a good guy; obviously his friends got it totally wrong. Tiny is beside himself that he misjudged his friend for so long. He can't even remember who told him that Alex was gay in the first place. But Alex doesn't go off with women after the shows, he never talks about women in fact, and Tiny as he puts it, put two and two together and came up with five.

He also explains that it was him, Tiny, who warned all the guys off around me. He was only trying to protect me, and hadn't got a clue Alex liked me. That's why Alex had been contacting me as James on the dating site. He wasn't breaking Tiny's rule, he was just waiting till the tour was over and he could approach me without betraying his friend.

"Why James?" I ask.

"It's his middle name. It was easier for him to approach you anonymously. He was scared you wouldn't feel the same and it would be less humiliating if you knocked him back and didn't know it was him."

I can understand that.

"I don't know what to do Tiny? Help me?" I beg.

Tiny looks at me. "Do you like him that way?"

"A lot" I nod my head as I answer.

"Then my advice sweet girl is go for it, see what happens. It might not work out, but then again it might. Life's too short. If you get a chance like this then seize it with both hands."

It's good advice. Tiny hesitates before asking the next question.

"Can I ask? Does it bother you that he's a stripper?" I take my time to think about it before I answer.

"If you'd asked me before I came on this tour if I'd date a stripper, I'd have said hell no. But you guys are different. I mean I wouldn't go near Guido with a barge pole, I'd be scared I'd catch something nasty, but I don't think of Alex as a stripper. He's more of a dancer to me. I've watched him rehearse. What he does is art, not sleaze."

Tiny lets out a breath of relief. "Then give it a shot girl. You're two of my favorite people. I think you'd be good together."

I give Tiny a hug as he leaves. I feel more settled now. More confident in what I'm about to do.

When I open the door to let him out I find Alex slumped against the wall next to my door.

"How long have you been there?" I ask.

"Since Tiny came in. I followed him down." He looks defeated.

"Oh." I don't know what else to say.

Suddenly a thought pops into my head. "If you're not gay then who was the skank leaving your room the other morning?" I remember back to the scantily clad female I'd seen leaving his room.

Alex looks confused for a moment, and then recognition lights up his features.

"She was here to do a sports massage. I was suffering a bit after spending so much time in the gym with you and Tiny." He smiles.

His smile lights up his whole face. His eyes sparkle when he smiles, and there's almost a dimple there as well.

Tiny lets out a forced cough, forcing my attention back to where we are, standing in the hall outside my room.

"I'll leave you two to it then." He pats Alex on the back and kisses me on the cheek before heading off to his room.

"You want to go for a walk and talk about this?" Alex asks. "We've got a little time before I need to be at the theater."

"Let me grab my bag." I quickly retrieve my bag from the room and meet Alex outside in the hallway. He reaches over to take my hand as we walk to the elevator. It's such a simple gesture, but it warms my heart.

CHAPTER FORTY ONE

Sally

We talk about everything, yet we talk about nothing. I couldn't tell you what we talked about, but by the end of it I feel a lot closer to Alex.

He understood when I asked if we could take this slowly. Despite us having known each other for weeks now, I feel like we've only just met. The guy I thought I knew doesn't exist.

Alex's character hasn't changed, but it's going to take my heart a while to understand that he actually could be mine if I want it.

Of course the hussy that is my inner voice is begging me to take him to bed now. I'm tempted. Very tempted. But I'd like to do this the old fashioned way, and take it slowly.

I look up and realize we're back at the hotel. The afternoon has gone too quickly.

"I know you want to take this slowly." Alex says. "But can I kiss you? I've wanted to kiss you for so long." God, my knickers are wet just listening to the way he said that.

"I think that would be nice." Nice? Nice? Sally Evans, I berate myself, kissing Alex is going to be way better than nice!

And it is. Alex leans in and kisses me, gently at first. It's a soft romantic kiss. I'm not sure who deepens it, but we quickly lose ourselves in each other. My hand reaches up to his head, drawing him closer. He pulls my lower lip into his mouth, biting down on it gently. I melt into him.

"Yo. Lovebirds. Come on, dinner's getting cold." Jackal calls from the doorway. Too soon Alex pulls his lips away from mine. I moan in disappointment.

"Don't worry, we'll continue this later." The promise in his eyes gives me hope.

"I look forward to it."

He draws my hand into his and guides us through to the bar where the rest of the guys are waiting.

There's various name calling and jeering, but as a whole the guys are pleased for us.

Guido still looks perplexed.

"So how the hell did you get a gay man to go straight Sally? I need to know that trick." Everyone breaks out in laughter at his naivety.

Alex just holds my hand tighter in his, whispering into my ear. "Later." The promise in his voice has me so wet I whisper back that I'm going to have to go back to my room and change my underwear before we head to the theater. I'm rewarded with a very uncomfortable expression on his face and smile smugly when I catch him adjusting the hard on in his trousers when he thinks no one is looking.

I'm definitely looking forward to the show being over tonight.

CHAPTER FORTY TWO

Alex

The show goes well. We're all on top form tonight and the audience loves it. I find myself glancing into the wings too often though. I need to keep checking that Sally is still there, that this is real.

The meet and greet seems to drag on forever tonight. There's the usual raucous behavior and crude commentary from the fans. Sally's face looks more pinched than normal every time one of the girls gets a little too close to me. I get it. I'd feel the same way if she had a group of men surrounding her.

She catches my eye and I mouth, "I'm all yours." She understands and smiles back at me, blowing me a kiss.

The girl in front of me turns her head to see who I'm talking to, and gives Sally a filthy look. I'm not having that and hurry her along the line up.

I'm relieved when we finally head backstage to the dressing rooms. The guys are still ribbing me a little, but it's all friendly banter, and they remain respectful of Sally. They've all become attached to her over the past few weeks. I'm not sure if she realizes she's now got a group of protective brothers in them.

Sally never comes in the dressing room after the time she found me with my trousers down. Instead she waits out by the stage door, chatting with the theater staff.

No matter which theater we're at she seems to build a rapport with them. Since this thing with her friend's husband we tend to make sure one of us is with her though. I know she gets wound up over it, but none of us want to see her hurt. She's told us over and over she's in no danger, but as I told her, better safe than sorry.

I've just fastened the laces on my trainers when I look up and realize we're all here. That means no one's out there with Sally. An uneasy feeling prickles my skin.

"Who's with Sally?" I shout, a little too harshly.

They look at each other, obviously all thinking that one of the others with her.

"I'm sure she'll be fine." Tiny assures me, but I can see the tight line of his mouth as he says it.

He pulls on his polo shirt, which strains at the seams over his large chest. He's the first out of the room.

"You seen Sally?" he asks Doris, one of the volunteer dressers who's been looking after us.

"She was out by the stage door love, it got a bit stuffy in here for us." She answers.

Tiny and I head for the stage door, and I can sense that the others aren't far behind me. There's no sign of her in any of the narrow corridors underneath the theater where the dressing rooms are so we head up to the corridor that takes us to the stage door.

She's not there either. Tiny rushes out the stage door before me and I hear him swear.

"Get your fucking hands off her now." What the hell?

I follow quickly behind and almost lose it when I see Sally tight in the grasp of a strange guy. Her face looks red and puffy, it dawns on me that he's hit her. Anger starts to cloud my vision as I head over to him, but Tiny gets there first.

"I said let go of her." Tiny bellows. Sally looks terrified. Meanwhile the guy holding her looks deranged. He's shaking her like she's a rag doll. He reaches to slap her again but before he can Tiny gets to him, drawing his arm around his back. There's a sickening crack. I think Tiny's dislocated his shoulder.

The guy howls out in pain and releases his hold on Sally who crumples to the ground, and I rush towards her.

"Call the police!" Someone shouts. Tiny has the guy down on the floor and is hitting him. Guido and Jackal are trying to pull him back before he kills him.

Sally is trembling. Her face is white and shaken, apart from the bruise that is already forming on her cheek. I growl under my breath.

"It's okay baby. I've got you." I tell her as Jonny comes up behind me.

"We've called an ambulance for her, just in case. The police are on their way as well." He squats down on the other side of Sally and pats her hand.

'You're going to be fine Sally. We're here for you." I can tell he's holding back the anger.

Guido and Jackal have managed to get Tiny off the guy, all three of them are standing guard around him, and he's not going anywhere soon. I think Tiny's knocked him unconscious.

The street lights up with the blue of the police car and ambulance that are pulling up.

It's a blur of activity. I almost lose it when the ambulance men attend to the guy who attacked Sally first. A young policewoman is trying to talk to Sally, and calm me down at the same time.

As Sally's only walking wounded she suggests that she takes her to the hospital in her police car. She wants to get her checked out and doesn't want her to have to wait for another ambulance to arrive.

I'm reluctant to let go of Sally, but it turns out that she's just as reluctant to let go of me.

We get into the back of the police car and Sally cuddles up close.

I don't know what the hell happened tonight, but I'm damned sure going to find out.

CHAPTER FORTY THREE

Sally

It was past three am before we all got back to the hotel. It wasn't just Alex and Tiny who refused to leave me alone there. All the guys turned up and sat out in the waiting room with me.

I felt a little guilty sitting there, like I was wasting the hospital's time. I've just got a few scrapes and bruises and a sprained shoulder after all, but the policewoman asked me to see it through. The medical report will help in their case against Gary.

I'd been standing in the corridor near the stage exit talking to Bert, the doorman. It was a little cooler up there than down in the basement rooms. Bert had been called away by one of the dressers to check something. It was fine. I was on my own but I was in the back stage are of the theater so felt safe.

I shouldn't have. Nor should I have ignored what I thought were the two sightings of Gary. It turns out he'd turned nasty when Ashley kicked him out. He'd gone back and beaten her up, so she was now pressing charges against him. He'd fled up north before the police could arrest him.

They think he's been stalking me for the last few shows, and just took his chance tonight when he found me unguarded for the first time.

I've apologized to the guys so many times tonight for not listening to them, nor taking their concerns seriously.

I've never been so scared as I was when Gary grabbed me. I don't know what happened to him but that wasn't the Gary I know and remember.

He looked almost maniacal. He hadn't shaved in a while, and looked unkempt and scruffy. The Gary I know would never have stepped foot out the door looking like that.

He kept telling me it was my fault his marriage was over and that I had to be punished.

It was probably only a matter of moments from being grabbed and taken outside to the guys showing up, yet it felt like it was all happening in slow motion.

It hurt like hell when he slapped me, but it woke me up and that's when I started to fight back.

There was talk of Tiny being charged with assault, apparently he knocked Gary cold and broke his jaw. Eric called a solicitor in and that soon seemed to bring the talk to an end. I was furious, how could they charge him when all he'd been doing was trying to save me.

I get that he maybe went a little overboard; he doesn't realize his own strength sometimes. But I won't be sorry that he hit Gary. The little shit got everything he deserved.

Alex didn't want me to ring Ashley but I had to. I was so relieved to hear her voice. She kept apologizing until I finally shouted at her to stop. She's got nothing to apologize for other than her crap taste in husbands. To be fair to her none of us ever saw the real Gary. Most of the time he was all sweetness and innocence. She's better off without him, and I for one am very happy he's spending the night handcuffed to a hospital bed before he's taken off to prison.

Alex hasn't left my side. I should feel suffocated by the attention, but I don't. With him here I feel safe.

I panicked when we got back to my hotel room. I didn't want to be alone. Alex must have sensed what I was thinking, as he offered to stay with me.

"No funny business mind you." He chastised me. Damn. That would have been fun. Not that I'm ready for that yet. "I'll just hold you tight, keep you safe from the nightmares." He whispered as he brushed a stray hair from my face, and kissed the place where it had been.

Alex was true to his word. He undressed down to his boxers, and scooted in beside me in the bed. It felt strange having a warm body beside me again after so long. It felt even stranger being drawn into his embrace. None of my previous partners ever showed that kind of affection to me.

I thought it would take me ages to fall asleep, that my mind would be in turmoil for hours. But there, safely nestled against Alex I fell asleep almost instantly.

CHAPTER FORTY FOUR

Sally

I woke from my nightmare too hot and confused. I was disorientated. When I felt the body behind me I panicked. My nightmare had been about Gary grabbing me.

"It's okay, you're safe." Alex whispers in my ear. I relax a little against him. Either that's one hell of a morning wood or he's pleased to see me.

I slowly reach my hand back, testing how far he'll let me go. I know from our conversation he's happy to wait for us to have sex. I need to spend more time with him, with us as a couple, before I'll feel comfortable with that. I'm normally quite prudish, but I can't stop myself. I want to pleasure him.

He draws in a gasp when he feels my hand over his boxers, but he doesn't stop me. Instead he just asks if I'm sure.

I don't answer him with words; I ease my hand into the top of his boxers instead. My eager boy pulls his boxers down and tosses them aside, allowing me unrestricted access.

He fills my hand. I draw my fingers up and down his length, loving the soft silky feel of him. It's not enough.

I turn in the bed, moving to sit astride his thighs. My shorts are high on my legs and my sleep vest sits low on my bust. Alex eyes me hungrily.

I fist him in my hand, moving up and down slowly. Tossing my sleep tousled hair over my shoulder I lean over and draw my tongue across his tip.

Alex moans. His greedy cock pushing closer against my mouth. Well, it would be rude to ignore him wouldn't it?

I slowly lave his cock with the tip of my tongue, up and down. When I get down to his balls I suck one of them into my mouth. He arches off the bed. I repeat the move, turning my attention to the other one. I draw my tongue back up his length, teasing his tip a little more, lapping up the drop of pre-come that sits there glistening at the top.

Alex groans again when I take his length into my mouth. I've never done this before. I've never wanted to. I just hope my inexperience doesn't show. I want to please Alex.

Alex lifts his hips up and down in time with my movements. One hand is in my hair, caressing my head. His other hand is by his side, clutching the sheet tightly.

"Oh God, Sally. That feels so good." I smile. Looks like I've got this right.

I can feel Alex tense beneath me. "You've got to stop Sally. I can't. I can't." I ignore Alex and carry on, moving my mouth faster, drawing him deeper.

Even though it's what I'd planned, I'm still shocked when he comes in my mouth, yet I manage to swallow it all down.

I sit up straighter on him, licking my lips. My god, I've turned into a hussy!

Alex is laid back, eyes closed, a look of total bliss on his face. I put that look there. That feels bloody amazing.

He opens his eyes and looks deep into mine.

"That was amazing." He grins. "But it's only fair that I return the favor."

Before I know what's happening Alex has flipped me onto my back and pulled off my sleep shorts.

His long fingers caress my thighs; my skin is tingling all over. Slowly he draws my thighs apart and moves his head down. He plants gentle kisses up and down my legs, each time getting closer and closer to my center. Just when I think I'm going to die from frustration his tongue enters me.

Jesus. Christ. I think I've died and gone to heaven. Before I know it he's brought me to an earth-shattering climax. If I didn't love this man before, then I sure as hell do now.

"Thank you." He tells me as he draws the cover over us and pulls me in close to him again. He's thanking me? I should be thanking him. That was the best-damned orgasm I've ever had.

I still want to wait before we have sex. But now I know that when we do, it will be absolutely amazing.

We fall asleep again, wrapped up in a tangle of limbs around each other.

CHAPTER FORTY FIVE

Sally

The knocking on the door wakes me from a blissful, dreamless sleep this time. Alex is still out of it so I grab my robe and go see who's trying to wake the dead.

It's Tiny. That figures. It's normally him or Alex banging on the door. I smile as I look back and see Alex sleeping in my bed.

"Hey girl, how are you this morning?" He pulls me into a hug.

"I'm fine, Tiny. I feel better than I have in a long time." I smile.

"Oh yeah?" Tiny looks from me to Alex on the bed, a knowing smirk on his face. I hit his chest but my hand just bounces off, he's so solid.

"It's not what you think you jerk." I laugh.

"Hate to disturb the peace but we head out in an hour. I know what you're like, you'll want a shower and to do your hair and all that other la di da crap you do."

He's just turning to leave when I utter a smart reply. "I can think of better ways to spend my hour!" He winks at me and walks off.

I can't believe I just said that. I feel like I should go and wash my mouth out. Please don't let me turn into one of those girls, the kind who comes to watch the shows and heckles all night.

I head into the shower. I'll wake Alex up when I get out. He should still have time to get ready.

There's a cold blast of air as the shower door opens, looks like Alex is already awake. In fact parts of him are very much awake and demanding attention.

We make it to the bus with less than five minutes to spare, but huge grins on our faces. It's amazing what you can do in a shower without actually having sex. I think we need to practice that a lot more.

The guys break out in wolf whistles and catcalls, which quickly abate when they see the look on my face. Or I thought it was the look on my face.

"Blimey girl." Jackal calls. "That's one hell of a black eye you're sporting today." I reach up and touch my cheek, drawing my hand away quickly as I feel the sting of the touch.

I'd been so distracted this morning that I hadn't thought to look in the mirror. Alex looks at me as though it's the first time he's seen it as well.

There's anger in his face.

Dan steps back onto the minibus having stashed the last of the luggage, and spots my face as well.

"Bloody hell what happened to you?" He looks outraged.

"It's a long story Dan." He spots my hand in Alex's and the outrage turns to a smile.

"As long as it has a happy ending Sally." I nod.

"Yeah. I think this story has a happy ending."

I settle into a seat at the front of the bus, Alex at my side and we start to tell Dan all about our adventures in Edinburgh.

CHAPTER FORTY SIX

Sally

The last week has flown by. It's feels like it's gone much quicker than the other weeks. But, it's been a week of sheer bliss.

The gym has been out of the question thanks to Gary spraining my shoulder, so Alex has spent the time with me just walking, chatting and getting to know each other better.

I've kept looking for jobs on the various online boards, but nothing has come up. Alex told me he's happy for me to move in with him and have a go at writing for a few months until I find something. I'm still not sure that I'm ready for that. He's made it clear I'd be moving into the spare room. He doesn't want me to feel any pressure.

We've pulled up outside the theater in York. It's the last night of the tour. We've just got time for a rehearsal before the doors open to the public. We all decided we'd rather set off this morning than drive through last night. It means none of us have had chance to go home yet. Home. I'm not sure my house feels like home anymore. Wherever I am with Alex feels more like home than anywhere else.

Tiny is a little nervous as his fiancée Alison will be in the audience tonight. Somehow, in all the time they've been together, she's never been to one of his shows. She's coming down before the start of the show to meet me for an early dinner, later we're going to sit together out in the audience. I can't wait to meet her. Alex's mother will also be with us. I'm a little more hesitant of meeting her though.

The boys are on fire during the rehearsal. The routines are looking better than ever. Perhaps it's being back on home ground, or maybe it's just relief that this grueling eight-week journey is coming to and end.

Eight weeks ago I had a job, a career I was proud of. I was given this assignment on pain of losing my job and against my objections. I never thought I'd grow to love these guys, or to respect the hard work that they put in. Now I feel like I can call them my friends. I know I've got a friend for life in Tiny. And Alex… I don't know what will happen for Alex, and me but I do know I'm looking forward to finding out.

"Hey Sally, come here and meet my main girl." Tiny calls me over. Alison is lovely, she's quite petite next to his large frame but they fit together well.

She's a teaching assistant if I remember correctly, but she doesn't look like any teaching assistant I ever remember. She's a stunner. I soon find out she's also quite charming.

We're heading out of the stage door to go over the road to The Lowther for something to eat when I hear a couple of women gossiping in front of the shows poster.
"Absolutely disgraceful." One of the women sneers.

"Bet they've got no morals either." Pipes in the other.

Tiny sees the look on my face and just mutters "Oh shit" under his breath. He's learned to recognize this look, and he's right not to interfere.

"Excuse me?" I call. The two women turn to look at me in surprise. "I'm sorry, I'm sure I'm mistaken, but I could have sworn I just heard you bitching about my friends. My friends, who you don't know. Who you can't possibly have met. Because if you had you'd realize just how wrong and narrow minded you are."

"Sally" Tiny tries to interrupt me but Alison puts her hand on his arm to silence him.

"You see I DO know these guys. I've been on the road with them for the last eight weeks." One of the women has such a sour expression on her face at my last remark. "Don't you dare choose to judge me you sour faced old cow. And don't you dare to judge my friends. They saved my life, did you know that?" I ask them. They look at me dumbfounded.

"No, you didn't. Because you know fuck all about them." One of them looks offended by my choice of language, but I continue.

"You stand there all prissy, and opinionated and yet you know none of the facts. You're judging a book by its cover and you are so wrong."

"Well. Humph. I mean, well." The stupid woman is finally lost for words.

"You see that guy there?" I point back to Tiny. "You owe him an apology, and his fiancée standing next to him. He's one of those guys you've just been slagging off."

The two women finally start to look embarrassed. They mutter an apology to Tiny that's barely audible before rushing off up the street to escape me.

Tiny breaks out into laughter just as Alex walks out of the stage door and asks what's going on.

"Alex, this girl here is a keeper. If you ever screw it up you'll have me to answer to mate." Tiny slaps him on the back before continuing over the road to the bar.

"What's that all about?" Alex asks me.

I'm still laughing myself. Eight weeks ago I'd have been standing agreeing with those women, who'd have thought today I'd be stood here arguing against them.

"I'll tell you later." I promise. "Now let's go meet your mother while I still have the nerve left to do it."

Alex draws me close. "You're not worried about meeting my Mum are you? Don't be daft. She'll love you." He tries to reassure me.

Yeah. Right. Like any sane woman isn't nervous about meeting her boyfriends mother for the first time. I still remember meeting my ex's mother. She spent our entire relationship looking down her nose at me, and taking every opportunity she could to remind me that I wasn't good enough for her precious son. Now why would I be worried about meeting anyone's mother?

CHAPTER FORTY SEVEN

Sally

I couldn't have been more wrong about Alex's mother. We hit it off immediately. She's lovely. We've been sitting making inappropriate comments about our boys all the way through the show.

Jed had agreed to bring the bike to the theater tonight as a favor to me, so Alex could do a repeat of my favorite routine. What can I say? Jed has a soft spot for me. He'd only been able to meet us at a few of the venues that were in travelling distance for him so this act hadn't been a part of all the shows.

Alex's mum just sat there, her jaw dropping throughout the routine. I sat there feeling my knickers getting wetter by the second. He so has to bring that outfit home with him.

"Bloody hell, I didn't realize he was that good." she whispers to me as the lights go off.

Alison is enjoying the show as well, although I can tell she's struggling as I do with the cat calling and heckling that surrounds us.

"Don't worry about it Alison." I reassure her. "It's you he chooses to go home with after the show, not them."

She smiles wanly at me. It'll take her a few shows to get used to it, and she will. I'm not quite there myself yet but it is getting easier. Especially when I know it's me that Alex waits by the stage door for at the end of each night.

The intro to the finale comes on. 'Cherry Pie' by Warrant. I love this song.

The guys bounce onto the stage in black cargo pants, skintight black vests that accentuate their abs and black bandanas.

This routine is the most athletic of the night. At one of the choruses they stand in a line and tear down the front of their t-shirts in unison, ripping them from their bodies and tossing them aside.

They fall face down to the floor, crossing to the front of the stage in a series of humps and thrusts. Every time Alex's hips grind into the stage I picture him grinding into me. Shit. I'm one lucky girl.

Alex and Tiny turn and blow kisses at Alison and me as they're singing along to 'sweet cherry pie'.

There's a scaffolding pole erected at the back across the width of the stage and Alex grabs it, swinging his whole body up and over it to another of the swinging choruses. It's like a routine you'd see a gymnast perform. His back is to the audience and the muscles ripple and glisten in the spotlights. Guido and Jackal use the guitar riff to show off their back flips, crossing the stage against each other. No matter how many times I watch this, I still think they're going to crash into each other, but they never do. It's choreographed to perfection.

It's one of the shortest songs in their routine, and it always seems to end far too quickly.

As the final 'Swing It' is heard the guys rip their trousers off. Their backs are to the audience, the spotlights focusing in on each of their glorious, toned and very naked arses before the stage goes black.

The crowd goes absolutely crazy, giving them a standing ovation. I turn to Alex's mum who has tears in her eyes.

"I'm so proud of him." She tells me, before giving me a very emotional hug.

I look at Alison who's absolutely beaming. "That was amazing."

I'm not sure that it's such a good idea for Alison to see the after crowd at one of these shows, even less so when it's on home territory, so I suggest we go wait over at the pub for them.

Luckily they agree. Judging by the comments I can hear around me it's going to be one of the hotter nights at the meet and greet. I don't want to see it either as I'm not sure I can keep my jealousy under control.

I'm still humming the last song; I can't get it out of my head, when the guys finally make it over to the pub. Alex flashes me that gorgeous smile of his and squishes in beside me on the bench seat.

"What did you think Mum?" He sounds like a little boy now; seeking his mother's approval, bless him.

"Babe, that was your best show yet. And that bike routine, well even I nearly wet my knickers and I'm your mother so I'm guessing poor Sally here needs to go home and change hers."

"Mum!" Alex exclaims. I'm too busy choking on my drink to say anything. I can't believe she just said that.

For some reason all eyes at the table have turned to me. Great. She was loud enough that everyone heard her. What am I supposed to say to that? I blush like a virgin.

"Well, I could do with freshening up." I try to sound sultry when I say it but it doesn't quite come out that way. Never mind, they're all too busy laughing along with me to notice.

Alex puts his arm around me, moving his mouth next to my ear. Fuck, that move always excites me. He doesn't nibble my ear though, and I'm about to be disappointed till I hear him whisper "I don't know about you, but I'm more than ready to take your sexy arse to bed."

I turn to him, a huge grin on my face.

"Only if you do it properly this time." I answer.

"What?" He looks shocked. "You mean?"

"Yes." I interrupt him. "I'm ready, take me home and fuck me lover boy."

Alex has such a shocked expression on his face I think I've blown it. That didn't sound sexy at all. I messed it up big time.

"You really mean it?" He asks again.

"Yes Alex, I really mean it. I want you to take me home and make love to me all night long, and then, when the sun comes up, I want you to do it all over again."

Eight weeks ago I was bored, lonely and in a job where no one respected me. Now here I am eight weeks later, with a band of friends who I know will fight for me, who have become like family. But most importantly, having seen him move that body on stage all night long, I'm with a man who I know is going to rock my world tonight, and every other night if I let him.

I don't know how long this is going to last, but I'll take what I can, for as long as I can.

Now if you'll excuse me, there's a hot as fuck guy standing by the door, waiting to take me home and make mad passionate love to me. I'm sure you understand.

EPILOGUE

Sally

As comfortable as I am with Alex, I'm nervous as hell as he shuts the front door behind us. I want this, but it's so long since I've played this game I feel like a total novice.

I know we've done pretty much everything BUT have sex this past week, we've explored every inch of each other's bodies. Still. I feel like an inexperienced virgin all over again.

Alex takes my bags and puts them in the spare room for now; I still haven't given him my answer as to whether I'm moving in or not. The rooms nice, there's plenty of space and such, but right now my mind is on other things.

Alex can tell I'm not concentrating, that I'm nervous.

"Sally, I'm not going to hurt you, or do anything you don't want. Don't be scared of me." He looks a little crestfallen as he says the words. I don't want him to feel like that.

"Oh Alex, I know you wouldn't. I'm just nervous. It's silly I know. It's just that this is so important to me and I don't want to disappoint you." I hang my head, embarrassed at how open I've just been.

Alex crosses the room to me. He lifts his hands and gently cradles my face with them. It's such a gentle gesture.

"We'll take this at your pace Sally. You're the one in control here." He offers.

"What if I didn't want to be in control?" I whisper. My inner voice spurring me on to try and ask for what I really want.

Alex looks a little confused for a moment.

"I don't suppose you still have those cuffs do you?" I rush out before common sense kicks in and stops me.

Alex looks shocked. Shit. I shouldn't have said it. I knew it. But wait. His face just lit up with that gorgeous smile of his.

"You want to try the cuffs? Baby, I've dreamed about you in my bed with those cuffs." He grins. Thank fuck. Looks like we've been having the same dreams then.

Alex takes my hand and slowly, walking backwards he leads me from the spare room. He hesitates outside a closed door.

"You sure you're ready for this? I know I am." He gestures down to the very obvious hard on that's tenting his pants. "But I don't want to rush you. I'm happy to wait for you."

I hesitate a moment. Yes. I want this more than anything right now.

"I'm ready Alex. I just don't want to disappoint you." I confess.

"Baby, you could never disappoint me. I promise you."

He opens the door and gently pulls me into his bedroom.

It's neat and tidy which is nothing less than I'd expect from Alex. The bed dominates the room. It's a King Size pine bed and looks heavy and solid. I smile when I spot the floral quilt. Alex sees the direction of my gaze and laughs.

"What can I say? My mother decorated for me once when I was on tour."

Alex takes my hand and guides me to sit on the edge of the bed. I'm still incredibly nervous. It's a huge step for me.

Alex takes my face in his hands again. His large hands are so gentle as they caress my cheek, one brushing a stray piece of hair away. He draws his thumb over my lips.

I open my mouth a little and wrap my lips around his thumb, sucking it into my mouth. Alex moans in pleasure. I know he's thinking of my mouth wrapping round his cock instead.

I reach down to unfasten Alex's jeans, reaching inside for my prize. I graze the tip of his cock with my fingernails. I love the sounds Alex makes when I touch him. I love the feel of him in my hand. The soft silk of his cock, or the hard steel of his abs.

Alex stands and undresses. It's not the slow, sensual strip he'd perform on stage. It's a hurried tossing of clothes to the floor. In some ways it's better watching this than him on stage, because this is for me. He doesn't do this for anyone else.

He stands before me naked. Fuck. I love his body. I crook my little finger and beckon him forward. His groin is level with my face and I can't resist. I reach out and take his gorgeous cock into my mouth.

Alex moans. Fuck. I almost come just listening to him.

He pulls away before I can make him come. I huff in protest.

"Not tonight baby. I want to come in you tonight. I want to hear you scream my name when I do." He pushes me back onto the bed, undressing me much more slowly than he undressed himself. His fingers graze my skin. Everywhere his touch goes I am on fire.

Pretty soon I'm naked. We fool around a little longer, pleasuring each other with our hands and our mouths.

Alex lifts up from me to reach over into a drawer in the bedside cabinet. I assume he's getting a condom out. My eyes go wide when I see that's not all he's removed.

In the glint of the moonlight from the window is a pair of silver cuffs. He looks at me nervously.

"You sure?" he asks, although my answer is obvious as I'm already moving into position.

I raise my hands above my head and Alex is gentle as he uses the cuffs to secure me to the headboard. As he's securing me his cock is teasing me. When he moves his cock trails across me, soft on my skin, yet creating a trail of fire. I want to reach out and take it in my hand again, but I can't now. It seems to heighten the excitement and anticipation.

Alex rolls the condom on and hovers over me. My body arches up to welcome him.

And that ladies and gentlemen is where our story ends.

For now.

All that's left for me to say is that yes, book sex does exist.

And it was fucking hot.

ACKNOWLEDGEMENTS

Firstly I need to thank my fabulous cover designer, Margreet Asselbergs. She took my imperfect vision and made it a reality. I love your work lady and look forward to meeting you soon to say thank you in person.

To Jane Mortensen. My first fan girl, you'll always have a special place in my heart, not just because you make the most kick ass book trailer videos, but also because you're always there for me. Thank you.

To Ellen, who gave me the phrase 'foo foo clenching', I bloody love that phrase, thank you x

To my amazing team of beta readers, some of you only came on board with this book, others were there from the beginning, but you all offer words of advice, spot my silly mistakes and none of you realize just how much you add to this writing journey. This book is here thanks to your support and encouragement, never underestimate the part that you have played in it. Thank you Emma, Jane, Angi, Elle, Nadia, Louise, Danni, Nikki, Angela, Vickie, Nessa, Claire, Ellen, Mel, Kelly and Lyndsey.

To my street team who go out of their way to pimp and promote me, it's very much appreciated.

To Clare Williams, who encouraged me to include a bike somewhere in the book, I hope you like the way I did it. Thank you for being there to support me.

To the bloggers who've supported me every step of the way. There are too many of you to name, but I couldn't do this without you. Thank you.

Lastly, but most importantly, thank you to my readers. I am honored every time someone reads my book, takes the time to leave a review and share their thoughts with me, even if they're not what I want to hear.

ABOUT THE AUTHOR

Passionate reader, blogger, publisher, and author. I love nothing more than helping other Indie authors publish their books be that reviewing, beta reading, formatting or proofreading.

I love erotic suspense that's well written and engages the reader, and I love promoting the heck out of it over on my book blog.

I'm a mother, but most of all I'm me!

STALK AVA MANELLO

Goodreads: https://www.goodreads.com/author/show/7873269.Ava_Manello

Facebook: http://www.facebook.com/avamanello

Website: http://www.avamanello.co.uk

Amazon: http://www.amazon.co.uk/Ava-Manello/e/B00JB8MNYS

Twitter: @avamanello

Made in the USA
Charleston, SC
14 August 2014